THE CUPID GUILD

THE COMPLETE SERIES

L. PENELOPE

Heartspell Media, LLC

www.heartspell.com

Cover design by L. Penelope

Ebook ISBN: 978-1-944744-20-5

Print ISBN: 978-1-944744-21-2

CONTENTS

THE CUPID MIXUP

THE CUPID GETAWAY

THE CUPID COMPLICATION

THE CUPID FIASCO

THE CUPID MIXUP

BOOK 1

The Montagne hotel might as well have been a castle, and he might as well have been the prince. I met him in the bar late one night and it was obvious he was too much for me — too handsome, too charming, too rich. And while I could pretend I was a princess for a night, at the stroke of midnight, I ran away without giving him my name. I didn't leave my shoe behind, but I might have just lost my heart.

Can the Cupid Guild help this modern-day Cinderella get her second chance?

A quick, sexy, standalone romance with a paranormal touch. The story first appeared in *Heart's Kiss* magazine, published as "Before I Go."

ONE

IF MOM WAS ALIVE, she never would have let me get on that plane. She would have yelled, cried, bribed and begged me to stay home. In that order. But she's gone, my credit card is that much closer to being maxed out, and I'm here.

Standing on one of those iconic San Francisco streets, at the top of a hill, the city ripples out around me. I've always wanted to come here. There's a buzz in the air you can sense through the pictures. I feel it now, though it might just be anger pulsing though my bloodstream.

Behind me, the automatic door clicks shut. I take a deep breath to clear my lungs of the cloying scents of death and antiseptic. Instead, I get a lungful of exhaust fumes from the ambulance idling at the curb. Do they just sit out here waiting for people to die?

Of course, that's the pot calling the kettle black. Isn't that what I'm doing?

I walk back to the Hotel Montagne. These two blocks are the only part of the city I've seen since I arrived two days ago. A well-to-do couple emerges from the building; the man holds the door for me. His wife is sleek and sparkly—diamond studs, necklace, bracelet, rings. I shrink inside the door, pulling my battered department store coat closer around me.

The gleaming lobby is a gallery of mirrors, marble and chrome, with strangely shaped furniture dotting the space. I keep my arms close to my body, so I don't sully anything with my fingerprints. I imagine a squadron of maids must lurk in the shadows, scampering out to dust and polish an object as soon as it's been touched. This is definitely the poshest place I've ever been.

The same day I received The Phone Call—the one that upset my quiet, meandering life and turned it into this exercise in futility—a gold and purple envelope covered in glitter arrived in the mail bearing a coupon for The Montagne. A very generous coupon for a very expensive boutique hotel two thousand miles away. Once I looked it up and found the place was two blocks from the nursing home, I thought the coincidence was just too much. For better or worse, my decision was made.

Mom's voice rang in my head as I paid for a mind bogglingly expensive plane ticket for the next day. She screeched at me all the way to the airport, quieting down once I'd actually boarded. She'd always been afraid to fly. Her voice has also been silent the entire time I've been here. Maybe the silence is a punishment from beyond.

Growing up, we only ever visited roadside motels. Mom would leave a husband or a boyfriend and we'd move in for what she said would be "just a couple of days," but inevitably turned into months. As funds dwindled, the quality of the places would deteriorate. But they were usually a welcome reprieve from wherever we'd just left.

Mom would get a kick out of this place.

"Welcome back to the Montagne," the desk clerk greets me with a smile. I smile back; everyone is so friendly. It's like they don't know I don't belong here. The paltry amount I'm paying doesn't even come close to what my stay must cost. But it's nice, for once, to not feel like the rich kids are looking down their nose at me. I even go so far as to wave at the clerk.

The click of my heels echoes in the empty lobby. I'm headed to the elevators, but the idea of being cooped up in another tiny room, albeit a gorgeously decorated one, does not appeal. The clerk is young and apple-cheeked and looks like he stepped out of a J. Crew catalog.

"Hi, is the bar still open?"

"Yes, it closes at one-thirty, ma'am."

I check my phone for the time, stunned that it's so late. The nurses never enforce the visiting hours in the hospice wing, and that place is like a casino—curtains drawn tight, no clocks on the walls. Maybe they don't want to rub it in to the dying people that life is going on without them.

I thank the clerk and change direction towards the small bar. It's more muted and comfortable looking than the lobby—less chrome, more leather. It's also currently empty, no patrons and no bartender. I settle in on a barstool and take off my coat. The hotel is pretty small. I figure the bartender will be back soon.

To pass the time, I scroll through my phone looking at the pictures I took today. An old man in a bed, tubes attached to his arms. He looks so harmless. The giant hands I remember from childhood are now shrunken and shriveled, like the rest of him. I click the phone off. Nothing about that man is harmless.

The anger creeps back and I'm eager for a drink to whittle away the tension in my neck and shoulders. I turn at the sound of footsteps behind me.

"You're not the bartender." It comes out more harshly than I mean it to.

The man in the entrance looks down at himself and then back at me, cracking a half-smile. "No, I don't think I am."

He's the picture of a modern rake. Tallish with a medium build, black jacket over a white shirt, top buttons undone, grin set to mischief. Dark eyes flash as they appraise me. Lean, sexy, dangerous.

I swallow as the energy in the room changes. This man is an electrical storm; I could swear the lights short out as he enters. He sits one barstool down from me and I stifle the urge to adjust my skirt where it's ridden up, exposing a tiny sliver of thigh. Though as he assesses me, I'm not sure whether I really want to pull the skirt down or slide it up and feel the heat of his gaze sizzle over my skin. The place between my thighs hums to life, and with a mouthwatering whiff of his cologne, a furnace switches on inside me.

Can you have a hot flash at twenty-six?

"So, this bar is missing one important element," he says, scanning the empty room. My heater cranks up another notch when his gaze comes back to me along with a high voltage smile.

He gets points for not staring at my chest, which is covered in a very modest V-neck sweater. His focus stays on my face with the intensity of a spotlight. I'm caught in the beam, hoping someone else comes in to divert his attention and spare me the scrutiny. But my skin tingles, and I may actually be starting to sweat.

I break our eye contact. Clear my throat. "Should we, um, alert the hotel staff? Perhaps the poor guy has met with foul play." I shift in my seat and re-cross my legs, tugging my skirt down in the process. Subtly swiping at my brow, I'm convinced I'm dripping like a hog, but my fingers come away dry.

"Maybe we should start a search." His eyes twinkle devilishly and he stands and leans over the bar. "He's not down there."

"Hmm," I say, swiveling on my stool, glad the focus is off me. I bend at the waist and look around. "Don't see him hiding under any tables."

He moves to the wall and peers behind the oversized flat-screen TV mounted there. "Not here either."

I shrug. "I think we've mounted a pretty exhaustive search, don't you?"

Hands in his pockets, he saunters over and stands next to me, his thigh brushing my knees. "So, what are you having, assuming a bartender does appear?"

I try to ignore his closeness. "Tea."

"Tea?" He raises an eyebrow. "Iced or—"

"Scalding, preferably. Yes, I'm one of those people who goes into a bar and orders tea. I'm a tea-drinking teetotaler, sad to say."

"I'd ask if you were the designated driver, but…" His lips are so sexy. A day's stubble dusts his face and I struggle to focus.

"Alcoholism runs in the family. So I just stay away."

"Ah," he rocks back on his heels nodding. I could be imagining a hint of respect in his eyes. "Well, I don't think this place will lose their liquor license if I make you a cup of tea."

"You?"

With a wink, he walks behind the bar like he owns it. I open my mouth to say something, then close it when he bends down to search the shelves, allowing me to appreciate certain of his, uh, assets. He catches me staring in the mirror and I look away. He chuckles and shakes his head, returning to his task, and produces a cup and saucer.

"Decaf?" He holds up a generic teabag.

"No, give me the good stuff."

"Long night ahead?"

"Long day behind me. But…" I look out the front window to the street beyond. The nursing home isn't visible from here, thankfully. "I don't think I'll be able to sleep much tonight." I face him again and catch the tail end of a somber expression on his face before he replaces it with a smile.

"One sleepless night, coming up." His tone is light, playful, but his words set off a firestorm of images in my head.

"Are you sure you should be back there? Doesn't it take some kind of training or a certificate to operate a bar?"

"Are you doubting my tea-making abilities?" He holds a hand to his heart and feigns shock. "I guarantee this will be the best cup of," he looks at the teabag, "generic black tea you've ever had."

He produces a container of sugar packets and a little bowl of creamer.

"No, thanks—I like it black." I catch the flicker of a question on his face. "Black and hot." His eyebrows shoot up. He didn't expect me to flirt back. Hell, I didn't expect it myself. But the distraction is nice. I allow my gaze to linger on his smooth, café au lait skin and, good God, those lips.

His voice, low like the purr of an engine, penetrates my haze. "What brings you to San Francisco?"

I sit back and pull out a sugar packet, just to feel it between my fingers. "My father is dying."

The words settle like stones on the counter between us. "I haven't seen him in close to fifteen years. He wasn't…" I shift in my seat. "He wasn't what you would call father of the year."

"I always wondered who these fathers of the year guys are and where they come from. I've never met any." His eyes are warm and he leans forward, bringing his head just a tiny bit closer to mine. I don't really believe he wants to hear my life story, but he's listening intently, so I keep talking.

"A social worker from the VA tracked me down as his next of kin when he was moved to the hospice." I flip the sugar packet over and over, the granules inside sliding with a whoosh. He reaches out, covering both of my hands with one of his, stilling my movements.

His skin is warm. The veins of his hand stand out in sharp relief. Strong fingers. Long. My skin, a few shades darker than his, hums in response. Neither of us moves, locked together, even the rise and fall of our chests in sync as we breathe.

I exhale to break the spell. "I bought a plane ticket the next day. Dropped everything. Granted, it wasn't much, but still, everything, to come out here and sit by the side of a man who…"

I shake my head, sliding my hands out from under his. They feel different after his touch. Like they're no longer a part of me, but part of this other woman who meets strange men in bars and opens her heart to them. I chance a glance, expecting him to be plotting an escape. He probably came in here for some harmless flirtation, maybe a hookup, and instead he finds…me.

He pours the boiling water into my mug, then pours another for himself before rounding the bar to sit directly next to me. His legs are long and our knees touch. This tiny point of contact crackles up my body. Why is he still here?

"Where's home?" he asks.

"Cincinnati."

"The 'Natti," he smiles, as if he has some fond memory of the town. Which I highly doubt. "And what do you do there?"

I chuckle. "Isn't that the question of the hour? I'm currently, as we like to say, in-between positions."

He grins, stirring two packets of sugar into his tea. "You're keeping your options open?"

"I'm not a flake. I work hard, mostly retail, I just haven't found my — thing. My last job was selling used cars."

He stops stirring for a moment, then resumes.

"It's okay to laugh."

"No, I'm just trying to picture it." He closes his eyes and tilts his head in a move I find completely adorable.

"Can I interest you in a lovely, pre-owned sedan? It only has two-hundred fifty thousand miles on it?" I shake my head and blow on my tea before taking a tentative sip. It isn't one of the fancier brands I splurge on even though I can't really afford them, but the hot liquid feels so good going down. It enters my bloodstream, unsnarling some of the knots and loosening me all over, the way I imagine alcohol might.

I didn't realize I'd closed my eyes, but when I open them he's staring at me, raw desire etched onto his face. It takes me aback. I'd thought he was intense before, but that was only a preview. He seems caught off-guard as well and focuses on his mug, taking too big a swallow for liquid that hot.

"Best you've ever had?" he says, wincing slightly.

I chuckle. "Like you need the ego boost. But, yes, it's the best I've ever had." I say it in a mock sexy voice, aiming for playful. He stares at my mouth, then takes another gulp.

"Careful," I say, as he winces again. "You need that tongue, am I right?"

He licks his lips and the energy in the room changes on a dime. The low crackle of attraction is now supercharged. I suddenly regret my attempts at flirtation. I am so far out of my league here. If I'd had any sense, I would have packed up and left when he first walked in. I'm a farm team kind of girl, and he is definitely major league.

My track record with the majors is pretty much a disaster. I tried it once, a long time ago and still bear the scars. Worse, they still hurt. So yeah, Cinderella may get a ticket to the ball, or a coupon as the case may be, and she may even dance with the prince, but that whole happily ever after scenario doesn't happen for girls whose childhood address was the Budget Inn. Princes don't want girls with my kind of baggage. It's certainly not Louis Vuitton.

I turn to face the counter, removing my leg from contact with his. The energy simmers back down to non-lethal levels and we're just two strangers drinking tea in a bar.

"Thanks." I sip the tea for a minute, then push away from the counter and stand, determined to leave before things get out of hand again.

"You're leaving?"

"It's quarter to two. I'm pretty sure this is last call." I drain the last drops from my cup. If I don't get away now I may end up doing something I regret. The last thing I need is more scars.

I'm turning to go when he touches my shoulder. I freeze. Everything inside me crackles like a live wire.

"I never got your name," he says, maintaining the contact. When I turn to him, his gaze is potent, but there's something else behind it. Something I can't define and don't want to.

My eyes drop to his lips. A vision of how the night could go runs on a projector in my head. I tell him my name, he tells me it's pretty. I'm pretty. Would I like to come up to his room, or could he come to mine? He has a wide selection of the finest soft drinks to tempt me with. I say yes, because, really—who wouldn't? And the night is amazing. Or not, but considering the sparks shooting from a simple touch through the polyester of my sweater, it'll be amazing.

And then, I'll start asking him questions. I won't be able to stop because I won't want him to leave, or for me to have to make the walk of shame. I'll pepper him with questions and I'll pretend they're just light, getting to know you chatter, but really I'll be gathering enough information to stalk him on Google later. I'll imagine we can start dating, a long-distance relationship from wherever he lives. Of course, I could barely afford to get here so there's no way I can handle a long-distance relationship and, geez, who said anything about a relationship anyway, wasn't this supposed to be a one night stand? He'll figure out I'm crazy. He'll figure out I have issues and realize that he's a prince, he doesn't need this shit.

I'll have memories of one night that will haunt me for years. Years of wondering, years of hoping, following his Facebook updates to find out when he changes his relationship status. When he gets married. How many kids he has. The topic of their first-grade science project.

I shiver as Trevor's face pops into my head. Specifically, the smile on his face in his wedding photo. He's looking at his wife like she's made of gold. I'd always wanted him to look at me that way. She's definitely princess material, she's even wearing a huge, poofy, princess dress.

The man in front of me is waiting for my answer. I can practically see the crown on his head. I shake my head. "Names are overrated."

His eyebrows shoot up.

"I'm not—this isn't a challenge. You seem," I rake my gaze over him searching for the right word. Incredibly sexy.

Gorgeous. Orgasm inducing. "Nice." I wince for him. "But, um, my life is just too complicated for names…and things. You know?"

He takes a step closer. So close our toes are almost touching. His hand on my shoulder occupies almost all of my attention. "So, no names. Maybe we could use code names, like call signs."

"Or superheroes?"

He grins. "What's your super power?"

"Trouble," I answer immediately.

"I was thinking you looked like trouble."

"You would not be wrong. What about you? What's your super power?"

He shrugs. "Amazing tea making?"

I laugh and despite my best efforts not to, reach out to straighten his already perfect collar. "You know, I think you're dangerous to a girl's health." I get trapped in his eyes. "Danger, that's what I'll call you."

"Danger and Trouble."

I release him, pulling out of his grip and backing away. Take a mental picture of him standing there. The desire to stay is so strong, I know I'm making the right decision to leave.

"A match made in heaven if I've ever heard one," he says.

I turn and walk away.

TWO

MY LEGS ARE LEADEN as I drag myself the short distance back to the hotel. Each step is agony. The bell of a streetcar chimes nearby. If I run, maybe I can catch it. Ride it to the end of the line. It must end at the ocean. I could just sit there and stare at the endless, black water. Let the lapping waves soothe the ache in my chest.

When I arrive, the Montagne's lobby is once again empty. With the hours I keep, I haven't seen many other guests. Either everyone here goes to bed early, or they're all out enjoying the nightlife.

The one guest I did meet has not been far from my mind all day.

I find myself moving towards the bar, unable to stop the forward motion of my feet. Once again no one seems to be manning the place. All the stools are empty and I pretend the disappointment I feel is something else. Exhaustion maybe. Why *would* he be here? And even if he was, it would be to pick up someone else. Someone new. After all, I blew him off.

"You're not the bartender," a voice calls out from a table at the side of the entrance. Dark eyes glint above a roguish grin.

Tonight he's in a pinkish shirt with a navy jacket and pants. It's sort of corporate and sort of hip and all the way sexy.

My mouth wants to smile, but I try to stifle it, resulting in a weird mouth dance that probably makes me look like I'm having a stroke.

Was he waiting for me?

"I've already done the search," he says, standing. "Just to save time."

"How thoughtful of you."

He approaches the stool he sat at last night. Once I get a whiff of cologne, my brain scrambles. I take a step back and walk behind the bar to get some space. But the counter between us might as well not exist. Even from several feet away he crowds me. His presence takes up all the space in the room, and singes me with combustible heat.

He leans forward, his forearms on the counter. "A cup of your finest tea, barkeep."

"At your service." I bow with a flourish and turn to search for the mugs, mindful not to bend at the waist and stick my ass in his line of sight. I've never been behind a bar before, but this one has little to no organization. The shelves are a riot of bottles, glasses, stacks of paper, napkins, jars and boxes.

"Need a hand?" His voice comes from directly beside me, causing little earthquakes to rattle inside my body.

I usher him forward with a sweep of my arm. "You're the professional, after all."

"Go on, have a seat. I've got this."

I most certainly should not have a seat. I should leave, go back to my tastefully decorated room, and go to sleep. But my butt hits the stool without protest. My butt is not interested in being anywhere else at the moment.

"How did it go today?"

I take a deep breath. Whatever polite non-answer I was going to give dies on my lips under the force of his expression of sincere concern. He seems worried about me. Like he cares. It leaves me so off-kilter I tell him the truth.

"His organs are shutting down. He's signed a 'do not resuscitate' order so it won't be long."

He frowns and puts two mugs on the counter.

"Part of me is relieved— the world is better off without him. But part of me wishes I'd gotten what I came for."

"What was it you came for?"

I stare at my hands. The middle three fingers are crooked from where my father slammed them in the bedroom door after I'd tried to run away from his fist. I catch Danger looking at the misshapen digits and form them into a fist. "I was looking for a reason why. Some kind of explanation. Something that would make it make sense. Why did he hate us? Why did he hate us so much?"

My hands are shaking so I slide them into my lap. "I think I came here believing that I had to forgive him before he died. My life has been stuck in so many ways. I watched this documentary about forgiving and moving on and when I got that phone call…. I thought I had to come here and try.

"But you know what he said, while he could still talk?" Danger's eyes are on me, they haven't left my face. He's listening. The words spill from me, providing way too much information, but he's really listening. "He said I should have stayed home." I meet his eyes as my voice starts to waiver.

"He wouldn't admit to anything. Said I was crazy, that he never hit me unless I deserved it. That my mother was—" I shake my head. Shrug. "So, maybe he was right. Maybe I should have stayed home."

A steaming cup of tea slides toward me. I wrap my hands around it, relishing the sting of the heat. The stool beside me shifts as he settles into it, and I shake off the melancholy.

"But enough of that. What about you, Danger? Why are you here?"

He stares at me for a long time before a slow smile spreads

across his face. He's going along with my change of subject, though I have the sense he wanted to say something else.

"I live here."

"Here as in San Francisco or here as in…"

"The Montagne."

"You can live here?"

He nods. "The top three floors are residential."

"Wow, so, why do you live in a hotel?"

He fidgets uncharacteristically, like this is a topic he's uncomfortable with. I can't imagine how expensive it must be to live in a place like this. I'm starting to feel like we're not just in two different leagues, we're playing two different sports.

"It's convenient. You pick up a phone and there's room service. Laundry and housekeeping are included. What's not to love?" His voice is light, but there's pain tucked away there in the words he's not saying.

"My room here is approximately the size of my car—it's gorgeous, I love it, but it's tiny. And normally way, way above my budget, but I got in on the special deal."

"I didn't know there was a special deal."

"Some place called Delilah's Travel Agency sent me a coupon in the mail. It was really weird—handwritten calligraphy on fancy paper—but I called and it was legit." I look around the space. "I guess it would be kind of nice to live here."

My gaze is on the ceiling when he reaches out to push a chunk of hair behind my ear. I gasp as his fingertips graze my sensitive skin. Close my eyes. The energy crackles between us like a lightning strike and I'm ready to forget about baseball, forget about royal hierarchies and years of social media stalking and just give in to the thrumming in my veins that's begging for more of his touch.

His thumb is skirting the edge of my bottom lip when a jangling sound draws our attention to the doorway. A young Asian woman in tuxedo pants, a white shirt and bow tie tears into the room like a Tasmanian devil. Her hair is in long purple dreadlocks pulled back in a ponytail and her makeup consists mostly of glitter.

"Ohmygosh! Customers! I didn't think anyone would be here so late, I just stepped out for a second to check my— Time works so differently here. Sorry, it's my first day and so I didn't realize—oh wow! You already have drinks, that's so crazy."

She whirls behind the bar, a tornado of sound with clanging bracelets and tiny bells woven into her hair.

"You're the bartender?" Danger asks.

"Yup," she nods, the movement causing a chorus of chimes.

"Do you have some ID?"

The girl pauses, her eyes growing wide before she plunges her hand into her pocket and rummages around. The slim pants couldn't hold much, but her arm disappears to the elbow before she pulls it back out, displaying a laminated ID swipe card with the logo of the hotel and a picture of her face.

He nods and sits back, though his brow is furrowed. "You can't abandon your post, you know. If you have to step out you should find someone to cover you."

I never asked him what he did, but he must manage people for a living. Although anybody who's ever had a job before should know not to just take off without telling someone.

"You guys are drinking tea, well, that's on the house, I assure you. I'll have them take it out of my check, don't worry. I'm really sorry. So where are you from? What do you do there? How do you like the hotel? Isn't it fab?"

Danger's frown deepens as he stares at the strange girl and I down the last swallow of my tea, seizing the moment of clarity. "I actually better get going. It's late." I stand and avoid looking at him.

"Thanks, come again!" The bartender says cheerily.

I walk out, trying to convince myself that I don't want him to follow me. It's ridiculous really, this attraction. What's the point of feeling so drawn to someone you can never really have?

Someone who could only pile one more hurt on top of so many others?

"Trouble," he says. I keep walking to the elevator, but stop before pushing the button. I fish my key card from my purse then turn to him, not sure of what to say. We stand there like that, just staring at each other, until a Financial District type—slicked-back hair, power suit—comes up and stabs the button several times.

When the elevator dings open, we all pile in. The suit chooses the second floor. Danger gives me a look that says, *What, he couldn't take one flight of stairs?* I can't help breaking into a grin. I was thinking the same thing. When the doors shut after the suit's exit, the elevator doesn't move. We haven't picked another floor yet.

I step back and lean against the wall. Take a deep breath. He crosses his arms and leans next to me. We stand in the immobile elevator playing this strange game of chicken.

He looks like he's got all the time in the world. Doesn't touch me. Doesn't say anything, but the closeness of him in this tiny space makes the attraction from earlier seem like a mere sparkler. We have now entered the extended grand finale. 3D images are being created with the fireworks going off between us.

I shoot him a dirty look from the corner of my eye. His smile does nothing but grow wider. Damn those damn sexy lips.

I punch the button for the fourth floor. When the elevator arrives, I stomp out, not surprised when he follows. I spin around. "I'm not inviting you in."

"I didn't ask to come in. I'm just escorting to your room to make sure you get there safely."

"Is this a dangerous hotel?"

"You never know." He's smug and sure of himself, but, amazingly, not in an obnoxious way. His hands are in his pockets and he starts to *whistle*. What a bastard. Who does he think he is?

We stop at my door and I'm ready to say goodnight. Ready to banish him to the farthest reaches of space, where he can invade some other poor woman's psyche with his flashing eyes and strong hands.

He lifts my hand and brings it to his lips. "Have a good night, Trouble."

The fireworks have become a full-scale nuclear explosion. He releases my hand. Backs away.

Shit.

I hate baseball.

"Hey, Danger?"

"Yes."

"Come here."

THREE

I BACK INTO THE ROOM, my eyes never leaving his as he closes the door. The lights are off, but the ultra-bright street lamp spears the room through the oversized window, creating harsh shadows. My heart races so fast it makes me dizzy. I wobble when the backs of my legs hit the bed. And then he's all around me, his hands drawing my face in, his lips singeing mine with a four-alarm kiss. I seriously think I may spontaneously combust right here.

I tilt my head, drawing him deeper, pressing myself against the hardness of his body to feel the strength underneath the expensive clothes. My hands slide down and I pull him closer. He comes up for breath and, with a mischievous look, picks me up, palming my ass in his grip. My skirt slides up, legs wrap around him. I think he's going to lay me on the bed, but he turns and my back hits the wall before he attacks me with another searing kiss.

My lungs don't work and my brain has abandoned me, leaving me with only nerve endings on fire from his touch. The ache between my thighs pulses hotter and harder. He presses open mouthed kisses on the heated flesh of my neck, but I grab his head and pull him away.

"Bed. Now."

He grins and we spin around, then I'm spread across the bed and he's on top of me. I wriggle, struggling to get out of my clothes. My skirt finally comes off, revealing plain cotton panties, but at least I brought my good bra with me. He's only halfway out of his shirt when he stops, and I think something's wrong.

"What?" The panties can't be *that* bad.

"Nothing. You're gorgeous." His stare is appreciative, but it's like he's not even looking at me, he's looking into me. It's a little too much, so I grab his belt and start to pull. He brushes my hands away and makes quick work of slipping out of his clothes.

Black boxer briefs highlight how happy he is to see me. And this man's chest belongs on the cover of a fitness magazine. I run a hand over the planes of sculpted muscle. Just for tonight I've been called up to the majors. I hope I don't embarrass myself.

Needing to taste him, I close the distance between us. I moan as my lips and tongue run over his skin. He hisses when I scrape his nipple with my teeth. I bite down a little and he jerks, tries to push me away, but I don't move. I palm his erection through his underwear, just starting to get the feel of it when he tosses me down with lightning quickness and shifts the lace of my bra cups out of the way to lave my breasts with his tongue.

This position puts him right where I want him, his cock rubbing against my drenched panties, the blunt head stoking my fires. Proving himself a pro, he undoes my bra clasp, one-handed. My back arches at the unfettered contact as he kneads and licks his way across my chest. He flicks my nipple, then rolls it between his fingers and I feel close. The pent-up attraction is ready to overflow.

"Condom," I breathe into his ear and he rises and sheaths himself while I get rid of the panties. I rise to my hands and knees and turn to look at him over my shoulder. I'm burning so much for him that any position will do as long as he's inside me immediately.

He slides his hands over my ass, squeezing each cheek before flipping me onto my back again. He kisses the questioning look off my face.

"I want to look at you. I want to see what you like. I want to see your face when I make you come." He rubs the head of his dick against me once then slides all the way home, spreading and filling me, turning the fire into an inferno.

Painstakingly slow strokes have me thrashing around, begging him to go faster, harder, turning me crazy. I see the moment his control breaks and he slams into me, burying himself all the way inside as our pelvises smack together.

I shiver as sensation consumes me, turn my head away as his powerful strokes turn me into jelly. He caresses my face gently, turning my head even as his body pummels into me. "Look at me," he insists.

My eyes flutter open then closed. I struggle to meet his eyes.

He kisses me again, deeply, eyes open, and a fire hose of emotion blasts me. The intensity of eyes-open sex is beyond what I can even process. I can't believe I've never done this before. My gaze glides down to where our bodies meet, him pistoning inside me, the friction and slide pushing me over the edge.

It occurs to me that he's a stranger, but he doesn't feel like one, wringing every last drop of pleasure from my body. Something about looking into his eyes while he comes—you can't hide anything in that moment. You're not in control and whatever mask you're wearing slips away. What I see in that moment is all sincerity. There's no mask—it's a revelation I don't have time to ponder because then my own orgasm crashes into me, lifting my back off the bed with its strength. I can't help but close my eyes as it stretches on and on.

When it's over I lay there shaking, embarrassed as tears pool in my eyes. I can't be one of those women who cries after sex. Especially not after a *one night stand*. I turn away as he slides out of me and throws away the condom. In a second, he's back, wrapping his arms around me. Pulling me into his chest, accepting my random outburst of emotion.

I don't cry, I don't let myself, but I do take a moment to bask in the fantasy. How could this man, who doesn't know me, offer something so intimate? He's not yet on his way out the door, which is in itself surprising. Settling into his warmth, inhaling the clean scent of his sweat, I let myself imagine for a moment that life could be like this. That I could spend nights held safe in the arms of a man who loves me.

The thought shatters my daze. I shoot out of the bed on unsteady feet. Where the hell had that come from? He's looking at me like I'm freaking out, maybe because I am freaking out. I run to the bathroom and lock myself inside.

FOUR

I RUN the water in the sink for a long time, giving him a chance to make his exit. The shower is tempting, but I hate bathing at night. I'll need the water in the morning to help me wake up, and after all of this activity, I'll also need the hot steam to sooth my aching muscles.

After what I feel is approximately half an eternity, I wrap myself in the hotel robe and go back into the room. The fact that he's still here shouldn't surprise me. But it's not comforting, it's annoying and presumptuous. He should know how this goes down.

He has the nerve to grin at me when he hops up, still naked as the day he was born. His body crowds me in the tiny space between the bed and the dresser, but he doesn't touch me, just enters the bathroom. While he's in there, I fold his clothes into a neat pile and place them on his side of the bed. Just so he gets the message.

When he comes out he picks up the pile, sets in on the dresser and climbs back into bed, pulling up the covers. My look would turn him to ice if he were a normal human being. But he's steadily ignoring me. I'm just about to give him a piece of my mind when the phone rings.

It's almost two a.m. and my stomach clenches. He's sitting nearest the phone and picks it up, holding it out to me. His eyes are on me, but I think my face may have turned to stone.

I press the phone to my ear. "Hello?"

"Hello, Ms. Abernathy?"

I swallow. "Yes."

"This is Bayside Nursing Facility. I'm sorry to tell you that your father has passed away. The time of death was one fourteen a.m."

The room is quiet and the phone's receiver is loud. Danger can hear every word. He wraps an arm around me. I don't feel anything but cold.

"Thank you for letting me know."

"If you'd like to come in tomorrow to make arrangements—"

"No, I—I won't be making any arrangements. The social worker will handle whatever has to be done. Thank you. Good night."

"But Miss—"

I hand him the phone to hang up. He pulls me into the broadness of his chest and wraps both arms around me.

"I'm sorry."

"Don't be. I'm not. He was a miserable man. Don't waste any tears for him, I won't."

"I'm sorry for your loss." The way he enunciates each word, it's like he gets it. Like he understands that I didn't lose my father tonight. I lost him years ago. With every crack of the belt or blow from his fist, little by little I became fatherless. The scars I bear, both the ones that can be seen and traced with fingers and the ones deep inside are aching. But not because of tonight. Because of all the nights.

He strokes my hair and I melt into him.

"Tell me something," I say, wanting just a little more time inside the bubble of this fantasy. "Not your name, just something about you. Something you can't find on an internet search."

His hands stroke my shoulder for a moment. He kisses it, absently. It's a long time before he answers.

"I watched my mother die. She swallowed a bottle of painkillers right in front of me. She made me promise not to call for help."

I pull back and look at him. Here is the mask, for the first time. I can tell the difference between the him I've seen up until now and this—this is the face he wears for the world. I slide a hand behind his neck and pull his forehead down to meet mine.

"I kept the promise," he whispers. "Sat with her for hours. My father walked in and found us. He's hated me ever since. But she needed to go. He drove her crazy and she had to go. I couldn't save her."

"How old were you?"

"Thirteen."

"I'm sorry." I pull him into my arms. "I'm so sorry."

"He's well-respected—a self-made man, on the boards of charities, pictures with heads of state. And he's one of the worst men I know…. But everyone looks at me, hears my last name, and they see him." He tightens his grip on me. "I can't be anything like him."

He breathes into my neck and I shift my head. Our kiss is slow and from the heart. I taste tears and am not sure if they're mine or his. We soothe each other, hold each other, and my heart breaks for him.

I pull back and bite my lip. "You're something else, Danger. Do you know that?" I stroke his face, peering into dark eyes.

"Please tell me your name?" he asks.

My laugh is filled with tears and I shake my head. "I'm a mess. You do understand that? Not a cute scatterbrained mess, a real mess. Daddy issues, right? More baggage than you want to deal with. I promise you."

"You don't have a monopoly on baggage—"

"But it's different for guys. And men like you have options. I can tell you're one of the good ones. You don't have to settle for someone like me. You shouldn't."

"Settle? You're not settling. Why would you think that? Is it because of your father?"

I shake my head. "I just know." The look on his face tells me he needs more. I sigh and sit back.

"I had this boyfriend in high school. Trevor. He was the golden boy: popular, athletic, gorgeous. The world at his fingertips type—like you.

"My mom was a mess. She'd gotten remarried to another alcoholic, so home was a mess too and Trevor was like an island of calm in a torrential storm. I thought…. Well, I wasn't ready, you know? I just, I wanted more time before we had sex. But I guess he thought dating a girl from where I'm from meant a guaranteed score. When I wouldn't, he told me he couldn't deal with someone with so much baggage. All my issues were just too much for any guy with options. And then he left. He ended up marrying a cheerleader and has three kids."

I shrug. "At the end of the day you can't escape where you come from. My mom could never land anyone decent. Just once, I thought maybe I could break the mold. Fall a little further from the tree, but…I don't get to keep you. And pretty soon, you won't want to keep me."

"Shouldn't I be able to decide?"

I hold his eyes so he can see who I am. "I Am. A. Mess," I say slowly, so he understands.

"I don't exactly have *my* shit together. I don't even have an apartment."

"Yeah, you live in a hotel with rooms that cost more per night than one month of my rent. That's the definition of having your shit together."

He picks up a lock of my hair between two fingers. "You gonna try and kick me out again?"

"I'm leaving tomorrow." I check the clock. "Today, really.

Turning back into a pumpkin. Wouldn't it be easier to go now than in the morning?"

He releases my hair to run his fingers across my scalp. I close my eyes involuntarily as the sensation ripples through me. He kisses the shell of my ear.

"I can't go yet. If you kick me out now, I'll just camp outside your door like a stray puppy." He pushes the fabric of my robe down to kiss my shoulder. "There may be howling involved. I could wake the other guests. Do you want that on your conscience?"

I tilt my head to give him better access. He presses kisses to my neck, quickening my pulse. My breath hitches, becomes erratic as his hands slide down to my waist, shucking off the robe in the process.

"That certainly would be inconsiderate," I say, breathless.

"Let me stay the night, if only for the sake of everyone else. Think of it as community service." He pulls me into him, spreading my legs and reaching down to stroke the wetness there once, then twice, charging me up and leaving me ready to ignite.

"When you put it like that, how can I refuse?"

FIVE

I WAKE UP SURROUNDED in warmth, inhaling a lush, enticing aroma. The smell of man. I snuggle closer, still half-asleep, when a large hand palms my behind. Desire ripples through me and I shift, my movements tinged with soreness. Wincing open one eye, I'm greeted with his face, inches from my own.

He is so beautiful in sleep. He looks younger—that mischievous quality he often has about him is absent. Just a sleeping man, calm and kind. I move to roll out of bed, but he tightens his grip, unconsciously.

I can't believe I let him stay. Can't believe I told him about Trevor. Admitted to all of it. Though I didn't tell him about the internet stalking, or how, even now, I wish I had Trevor's life. What if I had said yes instead of no when he'd try to cajole me into bed? Would my life be charmed now? Or would he have still discarded me with the rest of the trash? And why do I still care?

Danger's lashes brush his cheek and a swell of emotion fills me to bursting. Last night was a fantasy. It doesn't even matter that in the harsh light of day he's even more beautiful than he was before. He's still a bubble about to burst.

As if he can read my thoughts, he opens his eyes.

"Good morning," I say and shift, trying to slide out of the bed. Once again his arms trap me back to his side. He kisses my neck and nestles in. I laugh and swat at him. "Time to get up, sleepyhead."

He groans in protest and refuses to release his grip on me. Finally, I worm my way out of his arms and go to the bathroom. When I come out, he's sprawled out across the entire bed grinning at me.

"What?"

"Nothing," he says.

"You look awfully pleased with yourself." I sit down beside him and he pulls me to him. "What if I am?" He continues looking at me significantly.

"What?"

"I'm waiting for you to say it."

"Say what?"

He just waggles his eyebrows in response. I rack my brain to figure out what he means, before a lightbulb clicks. "Best I've ever had?"

"Ahh!" he says, falling back on to the bed. "I knew it."

I turn to fully face him, growing serious. "Yeah, you are."

He sobers as well and reaches out to grab my hands. "I know you have your rules and everything but—"

I shake my head, pulling out of his grasp. "It was perfect. The perfect night. Now that the sun's up, I don't want to ruin it. Isn't it enough to be able to look back and have this one unspoiled thing to take with you? I guarantee if we try for more it will blow up in our faces."

I think he'll protest, try to make his case. I steel myself against his arguments, hoping he can just understand where I'm coming from. To my surprise, he nods and gets up. Puts his clothes back on. For a moment, I regret the covering of that gorgeous body.

He stands, fully dressed, looking at me through the mirror. I want to look away, but I can't. I owe him at least this much—to see him. His intensity is set to full blast, but his face is unreadable. He picks up a pen and scribbles on the hotel stationery, then seals it in the envelope.

"This is me." He holds up the envelope. "If you ever want to know who I am, want to get in contact, it's in here. Your choice."

A sharp longing pierces me as I look at the paper held in his long fingers.

"I need you to know that I do want more. I don't believe you're as much of a mess as you think you are. What I see is a beautiful, intelligent, strong woman who's been through some shit, and come out the other side. Not everybody does."

He places the envelope in the side pocket of my suitcase, then turns back to me.

"And for what it's worth, your high school boyfriend was a dick. And your dad. You don't have to believe anything either of them said. They weren't right. If you've had bad relationships, if you've chosen the wrong guys, that doesn't mean you don't deserve someone better. You absolutely do. Don't sell yourself short anymore."

He takes a step towards me, cupping my face in his hands before kissing me, hard and meaningfully, imprinting himself onto me. My eyes close involuntarily.

"You can't fix me," I whisper.

"I don't think you're broken."

I open my eyes when the door clicks shut.

I am alone again.

SIX

AN HOUR LATER, my return flight is booked and I'm ready to leave for the airport. I've already called my father's social worker—he'll be given a military burial in one of the available veteran's cemeteries. No way am I spending another dime on him.

There was judgment in her voice when I talked to her, but she only knew a dying old man. Letting go of any further responsibility for him feels good, not cold or callous. If there could have been reconciliation or forgiveness I would have been open to it. But there wasn't. I don't forgive him. And I'm okay with that.

A knock at the door startles me. My gaze lands on the envelope peeking out of my suitcase. I'd contemplated doing a dozen things with it: chucking it out the window, except the windows don't open; burning it, but I don't have any matches; flushing it down the toilet, but I don't want to create a clog. And, of course, opening it. Some part of me desperately wants to open it, to stay and spend another night in his arms. Over and over, I shake off the feeling, repeating to myself why it's better this way. I almost believe it.

I pad to the door and open it to find the bartender from last night, the odd girl with the bright purple hair. Today she's in a bellhop's uniform, complete with pillbox hat. A nametag on her jacket reads, "Delilah."

"Good morning," she says.

"Aren't you the bartender?"

"Yeah, that didn't work out so well. I think bellhopping is more my thing."

"But, I didn't call for a bellhop."

"Oh, you didn't?" She frowns. "So, you're not checking out?" Hope lights her face, like for some reason she wants me to stay. Maybe the work of being a bellhop doesn't appeal to her any more than bartending.

"No, I am checking out. But I only have one bag, I can get it."

"Oh, no, I insist," she says, barging into the room and over to the suitcase.

"Everything all zipped up?" she asks, running her hands across the green and pink floral fabric of my hideous discount bag. Her fingers brush the corner of the envelope, pushing it deeper into the pocket and zipping it up. She swings it off the luggage stand and carries it into the hall.

"I'll go ahead and take this down for you. It'll be waiting at the front desk."

And with that she's gone.

Standing alone in the room, I exhale, feeling like I just survived some kind of freak storm interrupting a quiet, sunny day. I do a final check of the room, stopping just short of sniffing the pillow he used.

Then I sniff it anyway. Try to memorize his scent. Grab my purse and head out.

For once, the lobby is teeming with activity. A family reunion, all wearing matching fluorescent t-shirts reading "The Hollisters — Building Our Legacy, Y'all," is checking out. They all have southern accents, and I bob and weave through huge teased bouffants and cowboy hats to get to the front desk.

"Sorry, sugah," a large woman says as she rolls a gold-trimmed suitcase over my foot.

The young man behind the front desk looks harried, but smiles warmly at me.

"Hi, the bellhop just brought my bag down, I'm checking out of 409."

"409," he repeats, clicking on the computer.

"Are you all short staffed?"

He grimaces. "A flu hit a bunch of the staff this week. Sorry if there was anything about your stay that was unsatisfactory."

"Oh no, my stay was delightful. I would definitely recommend the Montagne to anyone I know who could afford it."

The young man passes me my receipt and scans the bags behind the counter.

"What does your bag look like again?"

I look around. "You can't miss it—bright green. Looks like flower vomit."

The man frowns. "Let me check the back," he says and disappears behind a door marked STAFF.

A few minutes later he reappears with an older man in tow. "I'm sorry, ma'am, who did you say brought your bag down?"

"The bellhop. She was young, Asian, bright purple dreadlocks."

Both of their faces remain blank and a sinking feeling hits me. "Not ringing any bells?"

The manager looks at the desk clerk, then back at me. "No one by that description works on the staff of the Montagne."

"She was working the bar last night. She had an ID badge."

The manager kneads the bridge of his nose. "Jake, call the police, please." To me he says, "I'm so sorry ma'am, it seems you've been the victim of a theft."

I need to be at the airport in an hour. I've already paid a fortune for the tickets and can't afford a flight change fee. Fortunately, the cops come quickly. I give them my statement and a description of the woman. Then I'm headed back through the swamp of Hollisters to hail a cab.

I hadn't packed much for the trip. I wore the same skirt or slacks every day, dressing up in a vain attempt to present an air of respectability to my father. There were no valuables and the suitcase itself was no great loss, though it was new. The hotel promised to pay for the value of my belongings, but it won't be much.

I miss a step when it hits me that I had one priceless, irreplaceable item in that bag. I falter, trying to decide whether to go back to the front desk and ask them about all of their permanent residents. Will they tell me the identity of the gorgeous man with the sparkling, mischievous eyes?

The doorman waves me forward, holding a cab at the curb. I look back, through the sea of people. There's a man at the counter who could be him. Dark hair. Brown skin. Tall. I strain my neck to see.

Someone on the street honks, and I shake my head. Maybe this is a sign. I'm not supposed to know him. Contact him. Want him. Isn't this just what I wanted?

I climb into the cab. The door shuts, sealing me in. I look back as we pull away.

It's for the best.

It has to be.

SEVEN

FROM ACROSS AN IMMACULATE DESK, Delilah's supervisor, Neenah, stares her down. Delilah taps a glittering nail on her thigh, looking anywhere but her boss's iron gaze.

"Explain this to me again," Neenah says. "What am I looking at?"

Delilah takes a deep breath, a habit gleaned from living around humans for so long. Breathing usually helps her fit in better.

"He's logging in to the database to search the guest registry. But he always stops himself. Tells himself that if she'd wanted to contact him she would have."

"And how many times a day does he do this?"

Delilah sighs, another unnecessary action. "Several."

Neenah sets the tablet down gingerly, the live feed still playing. She straightens it into perfect alignment with the edge of the desk. "And how long has it been?"

Delilah looks at her bare wrist and tilts her head, counting. "Approximately 2 months, 3 weeks and 4 days. Time works differently over there, you have to realize."

Neenah shakes her head, causing the ruby-red hair she's

chosen for her human body to briefly shift back into her natural smoke-like form. When meeting with her subordinates, she usually matches the form they hold, though staying human is tricky without a great deal of practice—especially when strong emotions come into play.

For a second, she flickers into a murky haze, then comes back full force. "This is unacceptable. Why didn't you predict that she'd leave without her bag?"

Delilah picks at the polish on her nails and shrugs. "It was a miscalculation."

"And where is the suitcase in question?"

"Tech support is on it. They'll have it put back together really soon."

"How many dimensions did it end up in?"

"Only a few hundred."

Neenah blinks. Too slowly to really pass for human, but she's never spent any time in the human realm. Delilah wants to fidget in her seat, but stays still under the scrutiny.

"Your first assignment is hanging by a thread, Delilah. Your future in the Guild is in jeopardy if you don't fix this now."

"It could have happened to anyone."

"*Most* of our liaisons understand how trans-dimensional transportation works. And it didn't happen to anyone—it happened to you." Neenah stares her down. "Fix. This. Now!" Her voice reverberates through the office as she de-manifests into a plume of smoke.

EIGHT

THE COFFEE SHOP is nearly empty after the lunch rush. I crack my back and sit up from my laptop; take a moment to calm the jitters that always happen after I press send. I'd tweaked my resume for the millionth time and it's now on its way to yet another job prospect. I feel really good about this one. For starters, they have an office in San Francisco.

Closing the many tabs I have open in my browser, I stop at the one I can never bring myself to get rid of. The Montagne's website.

It's glossy and slick, just like the place itself. I've stared at the photo of the bar more times than I care to think about. I can picture just where he stood when he made me that first tea. Where I sat when he ran his fingertips across my face, moving my hair and emblazoning himself across my soul.

After a week back home, I called the hotel and tried to find him. But just as I thought, they don't give out personal information about their guests or permanent residents. It was a dead end, and short of hopping on a plane and sitting in the lobby until he appeared, I don't have any other way to figure out who he is. Once I get a job and can pay down my credit card, I can go back.

There's no guarantee that he'll be happy to see me or that he'll even be there, but the hope spreads out before me like something I can grasp. The hope is new.

I pack up my computer and wave goodbye to my favorite barista. Yes, I splurged on coffee today, and I don't even feel bad about it. I just have this feeling that everything is turning around. It's gorgeous out; I pause on the sidewalk just to feel the sun warm my face. There's this idea that's been forming inside me that things can be different. It's grabbed hold of that pessimist inside me and put her in a strangle hold. I don't know exactly where it came from, but sometimes it makes me giddy.

I think it's called happiness.

I don't really have any reason to be happy, but I am. Maybe it's the hope.

I make it only a block towards my apartment, when I hear someone calling my name. The familiar deep voice causes me to turn around slowly.

"It *is* you."

He hasn't changed a bit. Still cocky and self-assured, still just as handsome as I remember. Trevor stands before me, grinning widely.

"Hi," I say, a little in shock.

His perfect teeth sparkle with an almost feral quality.

"You're back in town," I say.

"Yeah, I'm here visiting my mom. She just had knee surgery, so I'm helping out." He lifts his pharmacy bag as proof.

I smile. Perfect son. Almost perfect boyfriend. But not quite.

The harsh light of day exposes bags under Trevor's eyes. He wears a polo shirt and khakis, the blandest clothes known to man. I shade my eyes from the sun's glare as I look up at him.

"How's your family? The wife? Kids?"

He looks down, the smile faltering a bit. "We're, um, we got separated a few months ago."

"Oh, I'm sorry to hear that," I say, really meaning it.

He shrugs, looking off down the street. "Yeah, well, it happens." He seems very blasé about the loss of his family. I mean, I wouldn't expect him to be crying in the street, but still, some emotion would be nice. "You know, we should go out some time. Catch up."

I freeze, not sure what I'm hearing. Is he asking me out? Is this really happening?

"Um, I haven't really kept in touch with many people from high school, but a bunch of folks are still in town. Maybe we could get a group together one night," I say. After years of longing, suddenly the thought of being alone with Trevor leaves me cold.

"No, I mean you and me." His hand snakes out to touch my arm before I can stop it. "You look really good. You haven't changed a bit."

His palm is cool and dry. Sort of reptilian.

"You and me?" I repeat, incredulous.

"Yeah," he shoots me with his biggest caliber grin. "We used to have fun together."

If by fun he means I used to let him stick his tongue down my throat and pry his hand out of my panties, then sure, I guess that was fun for him.

"You're right, I haven't changed. I still have the same baggage I did back then. Don't you remember, I had too many *issues* to deal with? You didn't have time for it then. Why would you now?"

His grin falls away. "Did I say that?"

I have to catch my mouth from falling open. "Yes, you did."

"Well, that was a long time ago." His eyes run appreciatively down my body not once, but twice. They get stuck on my breasts with each lap. This morning, when I put on the sundress and strappy sandals, I felt good. That hope had wormed its way into my mind again and I wanted to look nice, just because. But his eyes on me make me want to find a sweater and cover up.

Suddenly, I remember why I didn't want to sleep with him in the first place. It hadn't felt right. He hadn't been right. All these years I thought I'd missed out on someone wonderful. A perfect guy with a perfect life.

But Trevor isn't a prince. He never was.

I pick his hand off my arm and take a step back. "Sorry, I'm busy." I turn and walk off, swaying with every step just so he'll know what he's missing.

Everything that Danger told me suddenly clicks into place. I'd let Trevor's words hold so much power over me all these years. I thought he was the pinnacle, that it couldn't get any better than him. I've never been so happy to be wrong.

I round the corner to my apartment, still feeling on top of the world. Lost in thought, I notice someone standing outside the apartment doors, but don't really look at them until I bump into a pink and green floral suitcase sitting on the stoop.

"Ooh, I'm sorry. You know I had one just like—"

My jaw drops as mischievous eyes crinkle, grinning at me. He's in grey slacks and a black dress shirt, rolled up at the sleeves, the top two buttons undone. Sexier than ever, if that's even possible.

I swallow. We stand there for a few moments drinking in the sight of one another.

"Hi," I say.

"Hi."

"You brought my suitcase."

"The hotel apologizes profusely for losing it."

"The hotel? They make you work for room and board?"

He shrugs. "It's my hotel."

I blink. "*Your* hotel."

"I own it."

"Oh." Of course he does. He stuffs his hands in his pockets and jingles his keys. I've never seen him nervous before.

"I—I'm not trying to invade your privacy, I just thought you might need this back," he motions towards the bag.

"Where was it?" I ask, still dazed.

He shakes his head. "Just showed up one day, out of the blue. Sitting in the lobby. It was covered in glitter. Not sure what that was about." He takes a step towards me. "A hand delivery just felt like the right thing to do."

"A hand delivery?" I quirk an eyebrow. "Sounds like a good thing to do with your hands."

He's caught off guard by that, but then his face morphs into that dangerous one, the one that got me hooked that first night.

"Well, since you came all this way," I say, "I'm guessing you want a tip."

His eyes never leave my lips as I close the distance between us and rise, pressing my mouth against his. Nothing has changed, not the heat, not the intensity, not the driving desire that makes me forget for a moment that we are standing out in plain view, blocking the doors to my building.

The door opens. I don't know if someone's coming out or going in. All I can sense is him around me, and I can't wait to get him inside of me again. I pull away, breathless, panting, looking at my reflection in his eyes.

"So," he says, tightening his hold on me. "Can I finally tell you my name?"

"Later," I say. "I don't think I can hear anything you have to say while you're wearing this many clothes."

The door to the apartment building across the street shuts. Delilah rolls up her window and picks up her tablet, tapping out a message to send back to the office.

Within seconds, Neenah has sent her reply.

GOOD WORK. HERE ARE THE DETAILS OF YOUR NEXT ASSIGNMENT. DON'T SCREW IT UP.

. . .

Delilah punches in the coordinates on her slightly modified GPS system. Her vintage, purple Volkswagen Beetle roars to life and disappears in a waft of smoky, leaving behind the sound of bells.

THE CUPID GETAWAY

BOOK 2

When curiosity leads Renee to duck under the caution tape marking off the top floor of a college house party, she's not quite prepared to find Milo. The popular girl and the solitary boy couldn't be more different, so why does he make her broken heart feel whole again?

One night changes everything, but in the morning, the gulf between their lives looks impossible to cross. Can the Cupid Guild magnetize these opposites before their chance at a happily ever after runs out?

A quick, sexy, standalone romance with a paranormal touch. The story first appeared in *Heart's Kiss* magazine, under the title "Before I Fall."

ONE

HEAD POUNDING along with the bass line, Renee crossed the congested living room dance floor and disappeared into the darkened hallway. She was still sober and couldn't blame alcohol for the haze that covered her mind. In the shadows, a couple writhed in one another's arms. She looked away—they obviously didn't care about privacy, but maybe if she'd averted her eyes a few weeks ago, she wouldn't have discovered Khalil in basically the exact same position, sticking his tongue down another girl's throat.

Jesus, what if he was here?

Part of her had felt relief when she discovered them. Khalil's hands on her own body had never quite felt right. And his tongue caressing hers had never made her quiver the way she always hoped she would.

Oddly unsteady in her five-inch heels, she carefully negotiated the uneven wooden floor. This old Victorian on the edge of campus had seen better days. It had at least a dozen drafty rooms. Paint peeled from the walls in patches that looked like water damage. She hoped it wasn't mold.

Students carved up these houses and split the outrageous

rents among as many as ten people. They made great party houses now that so many of the fraternities were on lock down for hazing. This wasn't the same house in which she'd discovered Khalil playing tonsil tennis, but at a certain point, all the turrets and peaks ran together.

Thinking about all the parties she and Khalil had attended made Renee's stomach clench. Her heart wasn't broken, but her pride was. They'd been a super couple, that's the only reason she'd put up with his bullshit for so long. His heavy breaths always panting in her ear, the way his cold fingers slid up and down her skin. She shook off a chill thinking about it. She had no idea how she'd lasted almost a year with him. Whoever that skank was giving him mouth-to-mouth, she could have him.

But now Renee felt adrift. Their friends had intermingled and since Khalil was slightly more popular—being a starting attack on the lacrosse team—he trumped whatever Renee's family, looks, and reputation brought to the situation. Now, she'd been on her own for the past few weeks, something she wasn't accustomed to.

The thump of the beat made her head spin. Everywhere she turned there were people grinding, or making out, or playing some kind of drinking game. Instead of oblivion, tonight she craved something she couldn't quite put her finger on. She could have stayed home, but staring at the four walls of her single room for almost a month had gotten old. Being naturally social, she wanted to be around people—she just needed to figure out who, exactly.

An Asian girl with purple dreadlocks brushed by her, bumping her shoulder. "Sorry," the girl said, giggling. The little bells strung into her locks jingled merrily. Her purple, glittery eyeshadow matched her lipstick.

Renee took a step back. "It's okay."

The girl grinned and then raced up the steps in a cloud of fruit-scented shampoo.

"And I thought *my* heels were high," Renee muttered. But

her stilettos had nothing on the other girl's insane purple platform boots.

Renee looked up the darkened stairwell, then behind her at the party she didn't want to be at. After a moment's indecision, she climbed the creaking stairs. The old wood shifted worryingly under her feet.

She was disappointed to find the second floor only slightly less crowded. A line snaked out from the bathroom, and the distinctive sounds of people hooking up rang out behind at least two of the doors. Another staircase led to a third level, but the purple dreadlocked girl was marking it off with yellow police tape reading: CAUTION! DO NOT CROSS!

"What's up there?" Renee asked, craning her neck to peer up into the dark.

The girl turned and shrugged. "Dunno. But it must be something really bad considering the tape and all."

"But you just put the tape there." Renee pointed.

The girl scrunched her nose and tilted her head to the side. "Did I?"

"I just saw you." Renee turned to see if anyone else was hearing this, but nobody was paying attention to the two of them.

When she turned back around, the girl was gone.

There was no way Miss Dreadlocks could have gotten by Renee, who was standing directly in front of the steps. But she couldn't have gone up either, not in less than a second—not in those shoes, without making any noise, when every section of the floor in the house creaked. It was like she'd vanished into thin air.

Renee considered the tape. If nothing else, it should mean fewer people going up there. The most likely explanation—that didn't involve the girl beaming back onto the starship she probably arrived on—was that Miss Dreads' room was upstairs and she just didn't want anyone bothering her.

But Renee wasn't going to bother anyone. She was just going

to have a look around, maybe enjoy a little quiet for a few minutes and then head home.

She slipped off her shoes and ducked under the tape.

The third floor was small, there were only three doors off the hallway, and it was thankfully empty. She pushed the first door open to find a tiny bathroom, its sloping ceiling meant you'd have to either be really short to shower in here or be okay bending over and hunching down. But the porcelain pedestal sink looked original and so did the black and white tile, only slightly chipped.

There was a bottle of combination shampoo and conditioner in the shower and not much else. No evidence that a girl used this bathroom.

The second door off the hallway was missing a doorknob so she passed it on the way to the third. She paused outside, listening. The music from below still vibrated through the walls, but was muted up here, it could have been happening outside or down the street just as easily.

The curiosity that had overtaken her could be explained by the fact that she was a naturally nosy person. One of her nannies had nicknamed her Harriet, after Harriet the Spy, and Renee hadn't even protested.

So she blamed her natural inquisitiveness as the reason she turned the knob and pushed open the door.

From the corner of the stairwell, Delilah watches the human girl enter the bedroom. She has temporarily traded in her physical body, with all of its color and pretty decorations, for her natural form—a smoke-like wisp of elemental energy. Though she would much prefer to be purple, stealth is necessary to observe the progress of her mission. A disembodied wisp of colorful smoke would not be incognito.

Her first assignment for the Guild did not exactly go well.

Delilah can't afford another mistake, or the dream she's had since her inception of becoming a full-fledged member of the Cupid Guild will never come true.

The roll of yellow tape she acquired from the Requisitions Department hovers in the shadows next to her insubstantial body. At least she had anticipated her target's nature correctly. All the girl needed was a push. Delilah's elemental form cannot smile in satisfaction, though she imagines herself doing so.

Not until the bedroom door eventually closes does she fade into the darkness and leave.

TWO

MILO LOOKED up when the door opened. The lock had broken just that morning and he hadn't had a chance to fix it. He figured he'd be flooded with drunk kids busting into his room, but hadn't had any interruptions—until now.

The girl standing in his doorway didn't look smashed. Straightened, black hair fell past her shoulders and the dress she wore was form fitting, but not a cry for attention. She was barefoot, with vicious looking heels clutched in one hand, but she didn't wobble or sway. She just stared at him with wide eyes.

He had an assortment of sarcastic statements at the ready for these instances, but they all fell out of his head.

"The bathroom's across the hall." He pointed behind her. She looked over her shoulder then turned back and stepped fully into the room, closing the door. Milo's eyebrows shot up.

"Um, sorry to bother you," she said. She had a cheerleader quality about her—small bones with a perky nose, like an ebony-skinned pixie—but instead of the high-pitched, girly voice that her frame suggested, she spoke with a pleasant alto. He bet if she broke into song, she would enrapture any audience.

"But?" he asked.

"What?" She squinted.

"You're sorry to bother me, but you will anyway?"

She ducked her head, looking apologetic and he felt a little bad, but seriously, what was she doing barging into his room? He couldn't stop his roommates from hosting these crazy parties, but he'd learned after being in college for two years how to survive them. Just stay away.

"Why aren't you at the party?" she asked, inching closer. She didn't recognize him, that much was clear, so what was with her? Why was she even interested?

He shrugged. "Not my thing." He closed the book he'd been reading and turned fully to face her. "What about you?"

Her face shuttered. She was standing in the middle of the room looking lost—he wasn't sure why she was there but suddenly he didn't want her to go. He had an overwhelming need to know what had brought her here into his room in the middle of one of the campus's epic parties.

"It used to be my thing. But lately..." She shrugged and looked around, then sidled closer to his bookcase and pointed to the light switch next to it. "Do you mind?" she asked, but flipped the switch before he could answer. The overhead light came on, the one that flattened the entire room making every-thing looked washed out.

Milo popped up and flicked on the floor lamp, then went over and turned the overhead light back off. She stood next to him looking up and up. It was true he towered over most people, but he felt like a giant next to her. She must be a full foot shorter.

She smiled and bent down. When she rose back up she was much closer to his height—she'd put on her shoes. Though they still only brought her up to his chin.

"Renee." She held out her hand. He stared for a second before grabbing it. She shook his hand firmly and fireworks shot off under his skin. The sensation was so surprising, he took a step back. She tilted her head at him, and his face flamed. He cleared his throat and squeezed her hand again before letting go. No fireworks this time, maybe that was a low blood sugar thing.

"Milo."

Her face cracked into another grin. "Milo," she repeated. "Cool name."

"Thanks."

"Not boring and normal like Renee. When I was younger, I wanted to change my name to something more dramatic…"

"But?" He was suddenly interested in everything about her.

She shrugged, running her finger across the spines of the books on his shelf. "I couldn't think of anything. My parents wouldn't have let me anyway. Names have power they always said."

He watched with fascination as she traced his books. Her nails were sparkly and blue, but short, not the fake claws lots of girls wore. "Renee means reborn," he said. "It's a good name."

She looked up at him and he noticed her eyes were a clear light brown, lighter than her brown skin. He swallowed.

"What does Milo mean?"

"Nothing."

The corners of her lips turned up and her brow furrowed. Her expression was a contradiction, sort of the way she was shaping up to be. "It has to mean something."

He turned slightly so he wouldn't stare at her; for some reason he couldn't tear his eyes away and didn't want her to think he was a creeper. Though he felt like one. Especially since he'd do anything to keep her here longer, to talk to her more. The thought scared him.

"It's based on the name Miles, which means either soldier or merciful, but in and of itself it's sort of just made up."

"So you can make it mean whatever you want it to?"

"I guess. I never thought of it that way."

"What do you want it to mean?"

Stuffing his hands in his pockets, he leaned against the closet door. He stared into space but his gaze kept coming back to her, looking up at him. "I don't know. What do you think?"

She cocked her head to the side and placed a finger on her lips, scrutinizing him. What did she see? He was ridiculously tall, light-skinned, and curly haired. Nothing really special, nothing that stood out except maybe his height and he tended to slouch to make it less of an issue. His T-shirt and sweats weren't from any kind of designer. But this girl, this beautiful girl, kept staring at him like she was seeing something more. He had no idea what that could be.

"Milo," she said, her voice cutting through the silence like a knife impaling him. "I think it should mean *solitary scholar*."

A chill went through him. Maybe it wasn't profound—he *was* sitting in his room alone studying in the middle of a party—but it felt profound to him, like she'd seen something true about him, even if it was obvious.

He looked away from her crystal gaze. "Sounds about right." His cheeks heated and he hoped she didn't see. But most of all, he hoped she wouldn't leave.

He was blushing. It was the most adorable thing she'd ever seen. Actually, *he* was the most adorable thing she'd ever seen— he had this sort of shyness to him, that wasn't really shy. He didn't seem to have a problem talking to a strange girl who'd invaded his space, but there was something solitary about him.

That was really the best word for him. He wore aloneness like a cloak. She envied him while at the same time, felt sorry for him. But standing here talking with him was like being alone with someone in a way she'd never felt before.

She'd always been surrounded by people. As an only child, she'd never had the opportunity to be lonely because her parents were always bringing people around. Their employees and assistants, staff, party guests. Renee's house was a bustle of activity one hundred percent of the time and she'd copied that once she'd gotten to college. Surrounding herself with room-mates and girlfriends and then her boyfriend.

Khalil had come with ready-made friends and they had all become a huge crew. She never had a moment alone and hadn't minded. Or had she? Had she really felt suffocated by the only life she'd known? So suffocated that it was actually a relief discovering Khalil's infidelity.

Milo stood there awkwardly. Did she make him nervous? She certainly didn't want to.

A pulse of pain shot through her toes. She'd put on her shoes so as not to have to strain her neck looking at him, but now her feet hurt.

There were only two places to sit in the room, the chair at his desk and the bed. It was just a double bed, and she didn't see how he could fit in it. Maybe he just slept crossways. The thought made her giggle.

He raised his eyebrows and she tried to get herself together, but the giggles turned into a full laugh and soon she was cracking up so hard she bent over.

Milo was at her side with a hand at her elbow, leading her to the bed to sit down. Then he stood towering over her looking concerned.

"I'm okay. For god's sake, sit down."

He looked around like he wasn't sure where he should sit in his own room, so she slid over to make room on the bed for him. The expression on his face when he sat next to her was priceless —both frightened and pained. She wanted to package it up and save it for all time. She also felt bad for invading his space but no way was she leaving now.

For the first time in weeks, she felt comfortable. Both in her skin and in her solitude. Being alone wasn't so bad if you were with someone like Milo.

"I was laughing thinking about how you fit on this bed."

His confused expression sent her into a fit of giggles again.

She grabbed his arm once she'd collected herself. "How tall are you?"

"Six six," he said, looking at her like she was a little crazy. Maybe she was, she felt a little crazy.

"Do you, like, have to sleep diagonally?"

He looked at the bed then back at her and a grin spread across his face. "I just curl up. Isn't that how most people sleep?"

She tilted her head to look at him and shrugged. "I have no idea."

"Why is that so funny?" He didn't look annoyed just perplexed.

"Again, no idea. I'm sorry, I wasn't really laughing at you. I just…I haven't laughed in forever. Sorry." She was still touching his arm, and it was warm beneath her fingers. He was thin, being so tall, but not reedy. There was a cord of lean muscle beneath her fingertips that she had the sudden urge to stroke. She wanted to see him without his shirt on, she wanted to find out what he felt like, how hot his skin was and if she could make him moan. She really wanted to hear him moan.

An image of him crowded into that tiny shower popped into her head. Water on his body, muscles bunching as he crouched.

"What are you thinking about now?" he whispered. She didn't know how much of her thoughts had made their way to her face, but she was at a loss for words.

Gazing at him, she kept getting caught on his lips. They were full and kissable and suddenly she couldn't think of anything else. She leaned forward, his lips the only thing in her vision. But he backed away.

"Oh shit. I'm sorry." She shook her head, mortification spreading over her. "Fuck." She pulled her hand away and ran it through her hair before hiding her face.

"You have a girlfriend," she said at the same time he said, "Were you drinking?"

His expression was concerned, not angry. She checked her breath. "No, do I smell like alcohol?"

He shook his head.

"So why did you ask me that?"

"I don't know, for a second there you seemed…drunk?" He lifted a shoulder, his gaze on her lips as well.

Understanding dawned and she felt a rush of affection for him, even more than before. "So, I'd have to be drunk to kiss you?"

His eyes widened and his mouth opened but nothing came out.

"Do you have a girlfriend?"

He shook his head.

"You just don't want to kiss me?"

Once again, his eyes betrayed him by roaming to her lips and staying there. "It's not that."

"What is it?"

"I don't even know you."

"I'm Renee. I crossed the police tape to see what was up here that was so precious we weren't supposed to find it. I found you." She leaned into him and felt his breath on her cheek. He smelled like peppermint and it only made her want to kiss him more.

"Police tape?" His eyes were guileless, so open and innocent.

She waved the question away. "Don't ask." She wasn't sure what it was about him, but she wanted to find out. "So?"

"So?" he whispered, a hair's breadth away. It was like they were being towed together by an invisible line.

"Can I kiss you?" Her lips were nearly brushing his they were so close. The peppermint invaded her nostrils and somehow turned her on even more.

"If you want."

There was no distance to close. His lips on hers were warm and sensual. A trill rippled up her spine as they came together. She wrapped her arms around him; his hands moved tentatively to her waist. Sparks erupted under her skin where he touched her. Even through the fabric, his fingers felt right and strong. She slid over into his lap and straddled him. His shock transmitted through the kiss, but he recovered quickly and his palms slid down to cup her ass, bringing her closer. Now she was flush with his growing erection. He swelled against her panties, drawing a gasp from her.

Her dress had ridden up to her thighs leaving them cold, but the rest of her body was hot. He kissed like she imagined he did everything, with focus and deliberation. With one hundred percent of his of himself and extraordinary attention to detail. He was thorough. Her mouth was plundered. His tongue stroked hers so completely, it was like she'd never experienced a kiss before today—this was so different.

Heat shot through her and her exposed thighs finally warmed as the pressure of his hands on her ass increased when he tilted her down. Her back hit the mattress and he was on top of her, keeping the weight off her body with his knees. Legs wrapped around him, and the fever between her thighs was growing. She broke her mouth away and gasped for breath.

"Take off your shirt."

He licked his lips and rose to do as she asked. She missed his hands on her butt, but it was worth it when he lifted his shirt to reveal cords of lean muscle on his slim frame. She sat up, running her hands down his chest then kissed everywhere she could reach. And then she got what she wanted, a moan. A deep one pulled from his diaphragm that shot her panties with moisture. She smiled and kissed him again, challenging herself to make him do it again.

THREE

MILO HAD MADE out with a few girls—in the closet while playing Seven Minutes in Heaven, on couches in basement rec rooms, beneath the bleachers at high school dances. His freshman year, before he started avoiding large gatherings of people, he'd had too much to drink one night and made out with his roommate's sister, which had been a mistake.

But making out with Renee made him feel like whatever he'd been doing before should be classified as a different activity altogether. Her skin was so soft and smooth, she smelled like sunshine and happiness. He couldn't believe how responsive she was, her whole body shuddered when he touched her.

He drew back to look down at her, hair spread on his pillow, and took a mental picture. A part of him was convinced this was some kind of hallucination. He needed to remember it accurately once he returned to consciousness.

She smiled drowsily and he rested his head next to hers, breathing heavily. Within a few moments, she'd rolled into him, forcing him to lay on his back with her tucked under his arm.

She drew lazy circles on his chest with her blue-tipped fingernail. "So why don't you do parties? Don't you like fun?"

He lifted a lock of her dark hair and rubbed it between his fingers. "You got it, I hate fun. Death to all fun. What, do you think I'm the Grinch?"

She giggled and the sound shot through his bones, filling him with warmth.

"I like certain kinds of parties, but these huge, faceless crowds that invade every corner of the house, those aren't the right kind."

She turned on her side and looked up at him, her eyes bottomless and open. "So what kind of parties do you like?"

"Smaller ones. Where you can actually talk to people. Where you can dance without crashing into everyone, and hear each other, and get to know people."

"You dance?"

He shifted, cupping her shoulder and kissing the top of her head. Hoping to avoid the topic. But, of course, Renee was having none of that.

She hopped out of bed and held out her hands. "Dance with me."

The music from downstairs bled through the walls, a driving, EDM track he suspected you had to be on Molly to truly enjoy. "To this?" He shook his head.

"You don't have any music playing devices up here?" She turned on her heel and crossed to the desk, then bent to inspect the shelf under the window. He couldn't help but look at her ass, pointed in his direction, and suppressed a groan. His dick was still painfully hard and embarrassingly visible in his sweat pants.

She tossed a glance over her shoulder and smirked when she caught him staring. A snap of her fingers draw his attention back to her face. "You have vinyl?"

He nodded and sat up, scrubbing a hand over his face. Adjusting his pants as best he could, he rose and paced over to her.

She kneeled in front of the shelf full of records, flipping through them. "Why vinyl? Do you have a record player?"

He chuckled. "Of course I have a record player. You think these are decoration?"

"These aren't even new, they're antiques."

"They were my dad's."

When her gaze hit him, he realized he'd let too much emotion into his voice. This girl was perceptive as hell. He held his breath, waiting for her to ask, but after a few moments she went back to scrutinizing the albums.

"We can dance to this," she announced, holding up a sleeve featuring a woman looking out a window expressively.

Milo paused, surprised. This had been one of Dad's favorites. The model on the cover resembled his mother, and he remembered sneaking down the steps, long after he was supposed to be in bed, to spy on his parents dancing barefoot to this song in the kitchen.

He pulled the album from her hands and their fingers brushed. Though she'd touched far more of him, the contact still made his breath catch. To cover his reaction, he turned quickly and crossed to the stereo, which really was an antique, but it was his dad's too and he'd never give it up while it still played. Maybe not even afterwards.

The opening organ of Percy Sledge's "When a Man Loves a Woman" filled the little room. Renee's arms wrapped around his waist from behind. He turned into her embrace and slid his hands down her back.

"I should get my shoes," she said. Though she was pint-sized, she fit him perfectly. He shook his head. When she went to pull away, he grasped her waist and hauled her up. Her legs came around him, her arms circling his neck. Her body pressed against him was sweet agony, and they danced like that, her clinging to him, attached to him, chest to chest, heart to heart.

"See," he said into her hair. "This is my kind of party."

She laughed and squeezed him tighter. His hands grabbed her butt to keep her in place, and she sighed against his neck.

"Mine too," she whispered so soft he almost didn't hear.

Renee woke up warm. It was odd because she was never warm when she woke up alone, but a wall of heat burned at her side. She pried her eyes open to find the sun shining into her room from the wrong side—then last night came rushing back to her.

Milo was still asleep, his face slackened and peaceful and beautiful in the morning light. She couldn't see his hazel eyes, but his lips beckoned to her. She kissed him gently, and he smiled in his sleep.

Her bladder was full, so she slipped out of bed to the bathroom across the hall. The cold, wood floor stung the bottoms of her feet. She ran back into his room to find him rubbing his face, staring at the spot where she'd lain as if confused. A huge grin broke onto his face when he saw her.

"It's freezing in here in the morning," she said, rubbing her arms.

"Then come back to bed." He opened the covers to her. She dove in on top of him, settling into the warmth of his arms, resting her head on his chest.

"Sorry I conked out on you," he said.

She didn't know how long they'd danced. Record after record had gone by and she hadn't wanted to stop, but at some point they'd fallen onto the bed and, apparently, into comas.

An apology was written on his face and she kissed it away. "Milo. Why haven't we met before?"

He brushed a strand of hair off her forehead before tracing her lips with his finger. "Cause you're not real."

"I'm not?" She raised her eyebrows.

"Nope. Not real. Just an imaginary girl who showed up at my door last night trying to escape the best party of the year."

"That must make you imaginary, too." She trailed a finger up his chest then stroked the emerging stubble on his chin.

"Why? I'm not impossible."

"What makes you say that?"

He lifted his shoulders. "I'm just Milo."

"And I'm just Renee."

"No, there's no such thing. You're like the sun, full of light. I've seen you out there. You always have a bunch of people around you, hanging off everything you say. You have a campus radio show, you write for the newspaper, you feed homeless kids on the weekends. You're a force of nature, Renee."

"How do you know so much about me?" She tilted her head to regard him anew. Last night he hadn't given any indication that he recognized her. How had she not seen him before? She would have remembered someone like him, so tall and beautiful.

He shrugged.

"We've never had any classes together, have we?"

"Freshman English. Econ last semester."

"You were in my Econ class?" She was incredulous. He nodded. "With Professor Akanbe?"

"Yup." He smiled a half smile and looked away, his hold on her loosening.

She thought back. Khalil had been in that class with her and she'd been so wrapped up in him, so wrapped up in who they'd been she hadn't noticed anything outside that little world. Shame filled her.

"That just proves I'm real. I'm a jerk. I don't know how I couldn't have noticed you."

He'd grown far away. Even though she was right there with him, his heart only inches from her lips, he was retreating. She could feel it.

"Why would you have?" His voice was hushed.

She forced him to look at her, sliding a hand to cup his cheek. With an unwavering gaze, she kissed him, slowly, remembering their first kiss and how she'd never felt anything like it before. He kissed her back just as thoroughly as before, with just as much focus. It thrilled her. She would make sure he knew how real she thought he was.

She slid her hand underneath his boxers and stroked him. She kept stroking until his throat vibrated with a rumble that made her bones melt. Then he pulled his lips away.

"What?" she said, chest heaving.

He shook his head and before she knew it, she'd been flipped onto her back with him on top. She was still in the dress she'd worn all night. He slid up the skirt, hands grazing her thighs until her hem was at her waist and her panties were revealed. Then he kept pushing the dress up, helping her out of it until she lay in her bra and panties blushing under his perusal.

He didn't seem to know where to look first. He took her in with tiny darts of his eyes; an eternity passed before his mouth descended onto her breasts, pulling her nipple between his teeth with the fabric of her bra as a barrier. She shifted to undo the clasp, pulling it away from her body to give him better access.

He licked her nipple, then bit it gently and the sensation shot straight between her legs. She trembled with need as he savored her breasts with his tongue. Propped on one elbow, his other hand caressed the underside of her thigh, then pulled it around him as he leaned his weight into her, his erection pressing at her core.

She was aflame, the well of arousal running deep until she couldn't take it anymore. Ripping at the waistband of his boxers, she pulled them down along with his sweats, wanting him inside her so much she was unwilling to wait through any more foreplay. She was so wet, responding to his slow, methodical tongue which pulled pleasure from the deep recesses of her body.

"Condom. Now," she ordered. Eyes unfocused, he shifted to the nightstand and pulled out an unopened box. She tried to be patient as he ripped open a packet, but couldn't keep her hands off him. Her fingers roamed his chest, his back, his dick, before he swatted her hand away so he could sheath himself.

She swallowed as the cold air hit her wet nipples—wanting to pull him back down on top of her, inside of her and keep him there. Both her legs wrapped around him, she arched her back to get closer. All too slowly, he guided himself home. As he sunk in, a flutter built within her chest and needed to escape. She let out a sound she never had before as he seated himself all the way inside her. It was more battle cry than groan and vibrated in her throat as it came out.

Thankfully, Milo muted her with a kiss, his hands on her ass cheeks, spreading them apart as he drove into her. Though her eyes were open, she couldn't see anything. She could only feel the way he slid in and out, feel his fevered skin beneath her hands everywhere she touched. Hear their labored breaths mingling as they both struggled for air. The gentle roars escaping from him spurred her on. She clawed down his back, begging for more with her body, unable to speak coherently.

She reached up to grab the headboard and isolate the movement of her lower half, pushing up to meet him thrust for thrust, the trembling in her legs making its way up her body. Her hair even trembled.

The orgasm built from inside, nurtured by Milo's deep thrusts, which impaled her in the best possible way. He demanded more from her. The unassuming boy she'd stumbled upon, who'd focused on her exclusively, required that she meet his demands. She rose to the challenge. Right before she flew apart, her vision returned and she found his gaze on her. Tears sprang to her eyes and then she was subsumed in pleasure that was felt in each strand of her hair. It pulsed outward like a supernova, infinite energy and blinding light. A star being born inside her.

Milo's own shouts brought her back to herself. He shook above her and collapsed, mingling their sweat and breaths. Her body thought it had run a half-marathon. She'd never put this much effort into sex, though this hadn't been a chore—it was effortless—but took everything from her. She was stripped bare, literally and figuratively, and the look on Milo's face showed he was similarly affected.

She felt cracked open like an egg, like everything was seeping out of her and melting into goo right there on the bed. Though it was a long time before she could move, she knew she had to leave as soon as possible.

Milo saw things no one had seen before. His knowing gaze sent shivers through her spine, and she couldn't escape. Solitary scholar was right. He'd been studying her all night. Half of her wondered what he'd found, but the other half did not want to find out.

FOUR

RENEE WALKED through the campus in a fog, looking over her shoulder every other minute, sure she'd seen a glimpse of a tall form from the corner of her eye. But he was never there.

It was stupid. She was the one who had left. Crawled out of the warm, comfortable bed, afraid to admit how too much comfort was uncomfortable. In that moment, she couldn't handle whatever had just happened and thought it better to leave a one-night stand before she was asked to leave.

But would Milo have asked her to leave? She knew the answer in the marrow of her bones, but ignored it.

The cold seeped into her skin. She drew her coat closer and pulled out her hat, but it didn't help.

Khalil had always hated her hat, specifically he hated hat-head and wasn't that stupid? She used to walk around letting her head get cold because of someone else's preferences. But Khalil had also never looked so deeply within her that she felt exposed and vulnerable. She never would have thought she'd want that, until Milo.

The shiver that came over her was immune to wool and down lining. It was from the memory of his hands over her, gentle and exploring, testing her, requiring things she wasn't ready to give.

She ducked into the Communications building and took the elevator down to the basement. Right before she stepped into the campus radio station, her phone rang. She tensed—hope surging from some hidden place inside her. Had he found her number somehow? But no, it was her dad. Or rather his assistant, since he rarely had time to call.

"Hi, Gloria."

"Renee, how is everything?" Gloria's voice was warm but clipped. Dad kept her really busy, but she could always get anything Renee needed. Too bad she couldn't get her a new brain.

"Good, everything's good. What's up?"

"Haven't heard back from you about your parents' annual white party."

Renee sighed. Senator Brookes's charity event got a lot of press in the social pages and it always looked best if the whole family was in attendance. Renee paused, leaning against the wall, her head in her hand.

"I don't know if I can make it this year," she said, not knowing exactly why she was hesitant to go. The glamour and buzz of her parents' parties had always appealed to her—or had they?

She was struck by the thought that she'd rather hang out with Milo in his third-floor sanctuary than be at any party ever. But she pushed the idea from her mind. That wasn't her life— she was out in the world and not hidden away like a hermit.

Gloria exacted from her a strong promise to try, and Renee said she would.

"Glo," she said as the woman began to get off the call.

"Yes?"

"How are they?" Her voice caught in her throat. She hadn't spoken to either of her parents in weeks, only to their proxies— either Gloria or her mom's personal assistant, Dean.

"They're good."

"Of course they are." Renee hung up, sighing. The Senator and his wife were always good, no matter what.

Her radio show's producer, a senior who she wasn't sure ever left the station, greeted her when she entered. Renee sat at the board, staring at all the blinking lights, willing her stray thoughts into place. Over the course of the next hour, she played nothing but classic soul: Otis Redding, Sam Cooke, Wilson Pickett, Carla Thomas, Mary Wells.

She kept her banter light, even though her heart was heavy. When it came time to take listener requests, she perked up. Milo had known about her show. He didn't say he listened, but he might—and maybe he'd even call in? What would she do if she heard his voice live on the air?

But as the show came to a close with no calls from him, her spirits dimmed. She'd left after all. What did she expect?

She packed her bag as the outro ran, then slipped out of the studio passing the next host on the way in. He was a guy that had been in their circle of friends—he and Renee used to be cool. But he got Khalil in the breakup and now they didn't even speak.

Outside, she stopped to zip up her bag. Awareness tingled up her spine and she turned around slowly to look up, and up. She couldn't release the smile that wanted to form—anguish caught her in a stranglehold.

Milo stood next to the door to the stairwell. He looked just as he had in his room, hands stuffed in his pockets, shoulders hunched a little, his beautiful mouth twisted into a wry grin. But his eyes were sad.

Her body longed to launch herself at him, but she held back. His melancholy gaze was still sharp. He saw more than she wanted, and she longed to cover herself, to hide in the crowd the way she always did, avoiding the scrutiny.

"Hey," she said, stuffing her hands in her pockets, mimicking his stance. His face fell as he withdrew his hands. He thought she was mocking him.

"Hey."

Silence hung thickly between them. He was staring at a space behind her on the wall, a frown creasing his forehead. He pulled something from his pocket and held it out to her. "I guess you left this." He held out a tiny gold hoop earring.

She touched her earlobe. She could have sworn she put both of those earrings on this morning. And were those even the ones she'd worn to the party? But her left ear was bare.

When she reached out for it, Milo dropped the earring into her hand, careful not to touch her.

"Thanks." Their gazes locked, but she didn't know what else to say.

He shrugged. "No problem."

"Renee!" a voice called from behind her. She turned to find the station manager standing in the hallway. "I need to talk to you about next month's schedule."

"Okay, one sec," she said then turned back to Milo. But he was already half-way down the hall, making fast time with those impossibly long legs. Her heart sank, and she forced the tears back from her eyes.

Delilah's purple painted fingertips scratch at the fabric of her skirt. She smooths the material before brushing one of her long dreadlocks from her shoulder. When she looks up again, her supervisor, Neenah's, expression has not changed.

"You were doing so well," Neenah says, with a sigh. Delilah nods, she *had* been particularly pleased with herself.

"You'd done your research and executed a plan that was simple but effective."

Delilah smiles. "Humans are naturally curious, and often the ones who follow all the rules are the same ones who justify breaking them."

"Yes, yes, breaking the boy's lock and predicting that the girl would be compelled to cross the police tape was all fine. Unusual, but perfectly within regulations." Neenah's green eyes narrow. She's gotten the hang of taking on human form now and almost never slips into her elemental form unless she plans to. She's even mastered the art of controlling her facial expressions to convey specific meanings, like intimidation.

Neenah leans across her desk and motions to the tablet sitting there with the latest progress report on Delilah's mission. "But how long has it been since they last saw each other?"

"Well, technically Renee *saw* Milo yesterday coming out of the library. You see, I arranged a little accident to befall his laptop so he would be forced to—"

"Not. What. I. Meant."

Neenah's command of anger is also exemplary. Delilah blinks rapidly, almost without thinking. These motions have become second nature given all the time she's spent on Earth lately.

"It's been a week since I rematerialized her earring in his room," she offers.

"Your window of opportunity is narrowing." Neenah shakes her head, a little too jerkily to be considered natural. "Close this case in the next three days or you will be assigned a Field Coordinator."

Delilah's shudder is one hundred percent natural. "Yes, ma'am. I—I won't let you down."

Neenah nods and de-manifests, dissipating into column of smoke.

Delilah pulls the tablet toward her, and engages the communication mode. "Requisitions Department? Yes, I'm going to need a couple of invitations."

FIVE

RENEE DEBATED GOING TO HER PARENTS' white party up until the moment she got in her car and started the drive home. It wasn't like she was doing anything else, but the thought of being around so many people, of smiling and glad-handing and turning on the Renee Brookes the world expected to see was exhausting.

For the entire forty-five-minute drive, she considered turning around and heading back to her room on campus and spending the night with the Bennet sisters and Mr. Darcy. But she stayed the course, and all too soon she was pulling into her family's gated driveway.

Her mother's assistant, Dean, greeted her at the door. "You're late, and the missus is in a state."

"When is she not?" Renee responded with an eye roll.

Dean shrugged just as his cell phone rang. He shook his head and answered his Bluetooth all while shooing her up the stairs.

The decorators were putting the finishing touches on the house, fluffing flower arrangements, and hiding the cables for the festive but moody lighting they'd added. Mouthwatering scents wafted up from the kitchen, where the caterers were making their magic.

Renee's bedroom hadn't changed since she went away to college. The walls were plastered with photos of her and her friends—the people who constantly surrounded her all through school, but who she barely even talked to anymore. The images staring down at her only served to underscore the gnawing ache in her middle.

The grandfather clock struck. Guests would be arriving soon and Renee needed to get ready.

She'd picked out the dress months ago, when the idea of the party was still exciting and didn't fill her with dread. The vintage, off the shoulder gown was classy but still sexy, with pearl buttons and ivory lace covering the skirt. After pinning up her hair, she took a selfie, but wasn't sure what to do with it.

She wanted to send the photo to Milo. Would he like the dress? If she posted it online, would he see? Did he lurk on her Instagram account? She stared at her phone until the screen went off.

A knock at the door jerked her back to the present. She called out and Dean poked his head in and whistled. She smiled, giving him a little twirl.

"Honey, you look fierce tonight. Jaws will definitely drop." He squinted and tilted his head. "What's wrong, sweetie?"

Before she could answer, his cell phone rang again. Renee shook her head. "Nothing." The shrill ring tone set her teeth on edge and this time it was her doing the shooing.

"I'm fine, promise," she said. He gave her a long look before closing the door.

She turned to her vanity mirror. If she was going to get through this, she needed to put her game face on. She hefted her makeup kit onto the table and proceeded to paint on the perfect girl.

Fully armored and shielded with a thanks to whatever god had created Sephora, Renee went downstairs to face the firing squad. She was a bit more than fashionably late and was immediately set upon by family friends, important donors, respected constituents, and other guests, all cooing and telling her how happy they were to see her. She smiled and posed for pictures with people she didn't know. The responsibility of being a Brookes was so deeply ingrained, she did much of it on autopilot.

In fact, her whole life felt like it had been on autopilot since leaving Milo's room a week ago.

Her parents expertly flitted through the crowd. Through the mass of partygoers, she got brief glimpses of her father's distinguished, bald head and her mother's elegant coif, but didn't actually see them up close until the speech-slash-photo-op where the Senator thanked everyone for attending and spoke briefly about whatever charity this year's party supported. Refugees from a war-torn country or school lunches for deserving, but impoverished young children, or something. Renee's mind had wandered, though she made sure her smile was perfectly welded into place.

After the applause died down and the music started up again, her mother cornered her. She wasted no time with a greeting, gave no acknowledgement that this was the first time Mary Brookes had seen her daughter in months. She just went straight in to the topic on her mind.

"Honey, where's your date?"

Renee frowned. "Date?"

"That boy you were dating? Carl? Chris?"

"Khalil, mother." Saying his name didn't even bring the bile it used to. "And we're not dating anymore."

"Hmm." Her mother flashed a smile at a passing attendee and drew Renee a little closer. "I could have sworn he was on the guest list."

"I promise I didn't put him there." And neither Dean nor Gloria would have, Renee was sure of it.

Her mother waved her wrist around as if it made little difference, then dashed off when someone more important called her name. A sick feeling took hold in Renee's gut. She wasn't even surprised when she turned and saw Khalil coming toward her, walking with his usual swagger. Anger welled up inside.

"Renee," he said, greeting her like they were still friends, like they were still anything. She stalked away to the kitchen where the staff were preparing the dessert trays.

Khalil's presence behind her was wrong. She whirled to face him, taking in his handsome, bland features, wondering what had ever drawn her in. "What are you doing here?"

He grinned. "I got an invitation. Great party."

"Why did you even want to come?"

"The Brookes' annual white party? Who wouldn't want to come? Besides," he said, moving closer to stroke her cheek with an ice-cold finger. "I think we should clear up our little misunderstanding."

She jerked away but found herself backed against the counter. "What misunderstanding?" Her skin was literally crawling, trying to get away from him.

"The one where you thought that girl meant something to me. She didn't. It was just a fuck."

"And I was just your girlfriend. You don't get to fuck other girls when you have a girlfriend."

"Well, to be fair, I don't think we ever specified that."

Renee's eyes widened. "You can't be serious."

"But if that's the way you want to roll, then I can handle it. I promise, it will never happen again."

"Renee!" Someone called her name. She peered around Khalil to find a photographer pointing a lens at her. Why there was a photographer in the kitchen, she had no idea, but this particular paparazzo was familiar.

Though the camera covered the young woman's face, her purple dreadlocks were unmistakable.

Khalil stepped to Renee's side and put an arm around her. Though confusion swirled in her mind, the smile was automatic, ingrained from years of charm school and cotillions and that one summer her mother had believed models could be five feet four inches tall. Whenever a lens faced her, whenever anyone's attention was on her at all, she smiled. *I'm like a trained dog.*

"Great shot!" the strange photographer said and then turned to disappear back into the fray.

"Wait!" Renee called, too late. She started after her, but Khalil's hold on her shoulder pulled her back. His touch sat on her skin like cold grease. Then another thought stopped her short—what if Milo saw that picture? Suddenly, she feared she may throw up.

"So, baby," Khalil said, sliding his arm around her again, like he had for the pose.

She pulled away and turned on him. "Don't call me baby. We're never getting back together."

His brows drew down. "Why?"

She stepped as close to him as she could stand to whisper, " 'Cause you never gave me an orgasm I could feel in my hair, that's why." And then she walked out of the party and straight to her car.

SIX

IT HAD BEEN A WEEK, so Milo decided to wash his sheets. They didn't smell like her anymore and it was pathetic to keep sniffing, trying to catch a whiff of her scent in them. The house's washer worked only twenty-five percent of the time, so he headed out to the laundromat on the corner.

A few other students lounged in the chairs or laid across the wide tables, either studying or sleeping. The TV on the wall played the local news. As he filled his washers, the newscasters engaged in what they must have thought was witty banter. Milo was only half listening until the words "Senator Brookes' white party" pricked his eardrums.

He sat heavily, transfixed by the screen, as stills from the event rolled by. Not only were her parents black royalty, they also looked like movie stars. His breath caught in his chest when a photo featuring Renee popped up. The newscasters hurried on to the sports report, but Milo couldn't get the image of Renee out of his head.

It was almost easier to believe he'd made the whole thing up than think for a moment she had been with him last weekend, dancing to classic R&B from his dad's collection. If it had all been a figment of his imagination, then he just might be a creative genius. He should give up engineering and study art instead—painting, or maybe he could learn to play the saxophone. That way he could use the swept up pieces of his heart for something useful, not just pining over a girl who was never real in the first place.

When the laundry finished, he stuffed it back in the bag and headed home. The house was quiet, no parties tonight. A few roommates lazed on the couches downstairs, playing video games or texting. He almost wished for the chaos and the noise of the week before. It would have been a good distraction from sitting in his room alone—something that had never bothered him before. Not before she appeared in his doorway, like some kind of fallen angel.

He climbed to the third floor, vaguely aware of soft music coming from up there. Maybe from the phantom roommate who kept vampire hours. He pushed open his bedroom door—he should get around to fixing that lock—and stopped short.

Renee stood next to the record player in a heavenly white dress. If Milo had taken anything stronger than Ibuprofen that day, he would have thought he was on some kind of trip. Her expression was sheepish. She looked up at him through lowered eyelashes. He stepped fully into the room and dropped the laundry bag. And stared.

Her phone was plugged into the stereo. The song that had been playing ended abruptly and she was pulling up another. The opening chords of Sam Smith's "Stay With Me" filled the room and broke him out of his fog. He closed the door and crossed over to her, without feeling his feet move.

She swayed slightly, still in her angel dress, barefoot again, a pair of white heels next to his desk chair. She held out her hands and he grabbed hold of them, this time ready for the electricity that pulsed through him when their skin touched. He pulled her closer until her head rested on his chest.

And then they began to dance.

Every feeling he'd been trying not to feel for the past week came out full force, threatening to break him. When the song ended, he stepped back. She looked up, eyes overflowing with tears.

Milo cupped her face in his hands and brushed away the wetness with his thumbs. "I saw you on TV tonight."

A look of horror and regret crossed her face. "I don't know who invited him."

"Invited who?"

She shook her head. "My ex. I wasn't sure if you saw—if they showed…"

"No. I mean, I'm not sure. But that's not—"

"Listen Milo, I wanted to apologize. I'm not used to people really seeing me. Nobody ever seems to. There's this girl who's an extension of her parents' brand, whose picture gets in the paper but the caption only ever says 'and daughter'. You said I wasn't real—you were right."

Her tears came faster now, and shame punched him in the gut for the fact that he'd had any part in putting them there. "That's not what I meant."

"No, it's okay. I mean it's not, but you know that." She sniffed. "I left that day because it hurt too much, being seen. It felt like standing naked in the middle of campus."

He couldn't *not* pull her into his arms then. But she was still too far away, so he lifted her, and sat in the desk chair with her on his lap. "You weren't naked in the middle of campus, you were just naked with me."

That brought a little smile to her face. "I know. And…." She swallowed before meeting his eyes. "It's kind of the only way I want to be."

"Naked?"

She laughed and nodded. "With you."

Her eyes were hopeful, staring up at him. He was speechless. He leaned in to kiss her and fell all the way down. The kiss was slow, full of things unsaid. Full of hope and care and tenderness.

She rested soft against his chest. He held her tightly, breathing her in.

"So…" she said, tracing a pattern on the exposed skin of his neck.

"So?"

"About that naked part? Can we start now?"

He laughed and carried her to the bed.

Delilah backs away from the window and floats down to the ground. In a shadowy alley surrounded by trash cans, she transforms into her human form, scaring a patchy gray cat who squawks and bounds away.

"Sorry," she calls out, the bells in her hair tinkling merrily.

She approaches the purple Volkswagen Beetle parked on the corner and turns back to Milo's house with a smile. "I love my job," she says, before hopping into her car and driving off to her next assignment.

THE CUPID COMPLICATION

BOOK 3

This just might be the worst day of my life. I quit my job and walked out—without my purse, wallet, or keys. The good Samaritan who returns my stuff is none other than our friendly, neighborhood rock star. Did I say worst day? I meant best. But when this drummer's dreams for the future are more than I can give, will that leave us playing out of tune?

Can the Cupid Guild bring this musician and his muse together in sweet harmony?

A quick, standalone romance with a paranormal touch. The story first appeared in *Heart's Kiss* magazine, under the title "Before I Run."

ONE

MASCARA CAKED and streaked around my eyes, making me look like a weepy panda. I gather wads of public restroom tissue paper and nearly scrape off my skin trying to remove the excess makeup. Only marginally successful, I give up. Let's just call it the smoky eye look. I'm not pathetic, I'm fashionable.

Staring at myself in the mirror, I lift the hem of my shirt. The largest scar is a little over an inch long, almost, but not quite in the center of my belly, north of the navel. There are other, smaller scars, but the biggest one always catches my attention. It's angry and red. Not fully healed yet. Slightly raised and puckered and hideous.

I'll never wear a bikini again.

Not that I wore them before that often, but at least I had the option. Sure, I've gained a few pounds since hitting my thirties, but who hasn't? My hips are finally nicely rounded, having lost that flat, boyish look that comes from being tall and skinny. They aren't what I would call child-bearing hips, but then again, they don't need to be. Not anymore.

I drop my shirt back down and force a smile in the mirror,

still hanging on to that idea from some article I read a decade ago that said smiling at yourself makes you feel better.

It doesn't.

I square my shoulders and exit the bathroom into the quiet cafe.

Coffee Bar, as the original owner so creatively named it, is part coffee shop, part bar. It also houses a tiny bookshop and a performance space. It's the closest thing that our town has to nightlife or day life or any kind of life, and at ten a.m. Thursday morning, it's basically empty. Just me, Trudy behind the counter, and old Mr. Chee in the corner, dozing off.

Everyone else is at work. Or in school. I used to work in a school until about two hours ago but now I don't.

My best friend Trudy frowns at me. The steaming hot mocha latte she made isn't so steamy anymore, so she dumps it and whips up a fresh one without saying anything.

I smile, this one genuine. It makes my cheeks hurt, but I do it anyway because Trudy is amazing and let me sit here sobbing unintelligibly for the past half-hour while she plied me with caffeinated beverages that I haven't been able to drink.

But when she sets the mug in front of me this time, I wrap my hands around it, relishing the sting of heat against my palms. Trudy hitches a hand on her hip and tilts her head to the side as if to say, *Are you finally ready to talk?* Only she doesn't actually say anything, and I love her for that too.

I force words from my lips. "So, I quit."

She blinks. "Okaaaay."

"In the middle of class."

"Okaaaay."

"I was just standing there, my lesson plan ready, the bell had just stopped ringing. The kids were rowdy, as usual. I didn't try to coerce them into their seats or yell or anything. I just stood there."

I venture a sip of the latte. Trudy has sprinkled cinnamon on the top, just the way I like it. "This is good."

She rolls her eyes like it's a given, though owning a coffee shop is no guarantee you can make a decent latte.

"I stood there until some of them actually noticed me. A few even quieted down. Some were already asleep. The rest were on their phones." I stare into the remaining foam. "I just couldn't do it," I whisper.

"Maybe it's just too soon," Trudy says, reaching for my shoulder and giving it a comforting squeeze. "Going back to work this week might have been a mistake. Maybe you needed another few weeks. To recover."

I shake my head. "Another few weeks wouldn't help."

"So, what? You just walked out of the classroom?" She picks up her own mug of something way stronger than I can handle and sips it, scanning the shop just in case a customer has sneaked in during the past few minutes and she's missed it.

"I walked to the front office and told the secretary that I needed an emergency sub. And that I quit. And then I left." I look around. "I didn't even take my purse. It's still locked in the desk drawer. I walked here."

I put down the mug and drop my head to my hands. The bell over the door goes off.

"I'll get rid of them," Trudy says.

"You can't get rid of them, this is your livelihood. I'm not going anywhere. I don't have my keys."

"Oh, sweetie," she says, clucking. I hear her go over to the register to wait on the new customer, but my head is too heavy to lift right now.

Everyone always said that I should be a teacher. It was always: Oh, Charlotte, look how well she organizes the other kids. Such a good babysitter, such a good older sister. She'll be such a good mother someday.

There wasn't even a question when I finally got to college. I'd spent six years after high school working full-time and taking care of my little brother Mat, so you would think I'd have given plenty of thought to my major. And yet I still chose Education.

Teaching high school English had made sense. Until it didn't.

I place my hands on my stomach and breathe deeply. What's that thing they have you do in yoga? Lion breath? I never understood exactly how to go about it, but maybe I should give it another shot. Maybe if I breathed like a lion I could grow some courage.

"How do you feel?"

I startle at Trudy's presence behind me. I sit up and spin around on the stool to face her. "Physically, I'm okay. Not 100% yet, but that will take time. That's what the doctor and everyone on the internet says."

She purses her lips. "If you don't want to go back and get your keys from the school, just take mine and crash at my place for the rest of the day. I'll pick up your bag after I get off this afternoon."

I look around again. The coffee shop side of Coffee Bar is warm and inviting. There's a chess table in the corner, a dartboard hanging on the wall, and even an old school Ms. Pac-Man machine.

"I think I'll hang out here if it's okay with you." I rise, holding my mocha. "Just keep the caffeine coming and put it on my tab."

A hint of worry flashes in Trudy's eyes, but she nods. I head for the dart board, ready to work on my non-existent skills. At thirty-three with no man, no kids, and now no job, maybe I can get on the professional dart throwing circuit. I open the case with the little missiles and start throwing.

TWO

AFTER FAILING SPECTACULARLY to hit anything close to the bullseye on the dart board, I move my attention to Ms. Pac-Man —my sister in feminism, eater of dots, and vanquisher of ghosts. I could use a little of her focus and determination right now. I engage in full-scale combat against those little dots until my big mouthed champion starts getting shit done.

As the level changes, I look over at Trudy, trying to communicate via telepathy that another shot of caffeine would be a good idea right about now, but she's with a customer. My neck cracks as I do a swift double take. And stare. Shamelessly.

I get an eyeful of his profile, all honey gold complexion several shades darker than my own. Short, kinky, brown hair and week-old stubble. Tattoos peek out from under sleeves rolled up to his elbows. My ovaries remind me they're still intact. In fact, I'm pretty sure they just grew big Ms. Pac-Man mouths and started salivating. I blink a few times to clear my vision, but no, he's real, he's gorgeous, and he's looking right at me.

The 8-bit sounds of disappointment cause me to turn back to the arcade game. I was staring a bit too long and now I'm dead.

Of course. My options now are to try darts again or convince old Mr. Chee to emerge from his slumber and play chess with me. Or rather, teach me to play chess.

From the corner of my eye, I see the hot guy head away from the counter. I can't help looking over again to find Trudy smirking, the reason for which soon becomes clear when I realize the hot guy is heading right for me.

His eyes have a relaxed, bedroom quality to them. They're a beautiful, sparkling brown, and I get to inspect them in even greater detail because he's standing right in front of me.

"Charlotte?"

Oh dear God, his voice. He should carry around spare ladies' underwear to hand out to any adult, heterosexual woman he finds the need to speak to. Starting with me.

"Yes? Do I know you?" A question I already know the answer to because I do not have Alzheimer's and that is the only way I would have forgotten him.

He grins, and his smile is everything. "No. I'm Micah. Someone asked me to give this to you." He holds out my purse.

Somehow, I'd missed the fact that the gorgeous species of human male was carrying a large, black hobo bag. I pluck it from his hand and lift it up like I've never seen it before.

"That *is* yours, right?"

Imagine if melted chocolate and molten lava mixed and then a mad scientist ran the mixture through a machine that turned it into sound waves—that's his voice. His mouth curves into a smile, and I have to physically remove my eyeballs from his lips.

"Yes. Mine. Um…. Are you a teacher?" Another brilliant question for which I already know the answer.

"Former student. I was visiting Mr. Crescent in the music department when this woman came up to me and asked me to come here and give you this. Then she disappeared." His brow wrinkles adorably. "Like, really disappeared. Into thin air."

I stare at him for a second, and he stares back then raises his brows. "Maybe she was just really fast?" he says. "Or I could have had a mini-stroke."

"Or fallen asleep standing up?"

He chuckles, making me feel all fizzy. "I *am* sleep deprived."

"I wonder if she was the sub?" Though how could she have gotten my purse out of a locked drawer? Maintenance doesn't even have a key, which I sadly discovered early last year. Maybe she's a part-time sub, part-time locksmith? Or jewel thief. That would explain the disappearing act. Besides, it would take a master criminal to handle some of those children.

He stares at me with bright eyes, and I feel the need to talk. "I'm a teacher. Or I used to be. I quit this morning."

I wince, but to his credit, if he feels any kind of way about my oversharing, he hides it well. "Sounds like a really hard job. I know I could never do it."

"I used to like it. No, that's not true. I never liked it, I just thought I should. But life's too short for shoulds, you know?"

He raises his eyebrows and my face begins to heat. Fun fact: when I get embarrassed, my nose turns red, and when I get embarrassed in front of a hot guy, I go full-on Rudolph. The absolute last thing I want is to turn into one of Santa's little helpers in front of Hot Guy Micah.

"Anyway, sorry. Thank you. I should have thanked you. That was a really nice thing for you to do for a stranger."

His eyes dance. "My mom always said her purse was like her third arm. Wouldn't want a pretty lady out there walking around missing an arm." He smiles again, and I just know it's Christmas in October on my face right about now. But somehow, his smile makes me forget my nose, and my sudden, self-imposed unemployment, and also my good sense.

"Do you drink coffee?" I blurt out. "Trudy makes the best..." Wait, what am I doing? Sanity returns like a tidal wave. "Never mind. I'll let you get on with your day."

I clutch my purse to my chest and turn around, hoping to at

least make a smooth getaway. Possibly by tunneling through the laminate floor.

"What do you recommend?" Little vaporized bursts of chocolate lava float past my eardrums. They send a tingle down to my toes.

I spin back around very smoothly, not wobbling at all. "The mocha latte is fantastic."

THREE

MICAH STANDS at the counter ordering his drink. I perch at the edge of a chair a dozen feet away, leaning on the table in front of me, so caught up in the play of muscles across his back as they stretch the fabric of his rolled-up, long-sleeved t-shirt, that I don't hear the bell ring again, or sense the presence of another person until said person is standing right next to me clearing her throat in the most annoying of ways.

Phyllis Jones manages to elevate the act of throat clearing into passive aggressiveness personified. I have no idea how I was her friend for so long.

"Ahem."

If she thinks I'm going to ask her what's wrong, she has another think coming. Then Micah turns around and I want Jonesy far, far away from me.

"What?" I snap, looking up at her. She's as short and curvy as I am tall and lean. Her straight, black bob is the direct opposite of my highlighted, bronze curls. I'm basically the film negative version of her, so why Tanner would date both of us at the same time is a great mystery. Also, why, when she found out, she would continue to date him is another enigma. One that I've almost stopped wondering about over the past few months.

"I heard you quit today," she says. When we were friends, Jonesy's ability to know the latest gossip almost instantaneously had been amusing, now it's irritating. "Tell me it isn't true."

We haven't talked in months and I have no desire to tell her anything, true or otherwise. Of course, Micah chooses that moment to sit down across from me. Jonesy scrunches her pert little nose at him.

"Micah Green? What are you doing back in town?" She flips her hair and shifts her weight to draw attention to her butt.

Oh. My. God. Is she flirting with him?

"Just visiting." His face is neutral-pleasant. At least he doesn't seem to be flirting back.

"Are you here for your brother's birthday party? I heard your mom is going all out. But, I thought you were on a tour?"

I look up sharply. Micah's jaw clenches before he plasters on a fairly realistic imitation of a smile. "We had a little break, so I came home to see the fam."

"Are you in the military?" I ask, raking my gaze over him again. His hair is not regulation and the facial hair is a definite no-no.

His eyebrows shoot up, and Jonesy gives a derisive snort. "Our Char, always so clueless. Micah's the drummer of the band RiotSphere. They were on Jimmy Kimmel last month." She shakes her head as if my ignorance of that particular detail of pop culture is just too sad for words. "He was a couple years ahead of us in school and graduated with my sister."

"Oh," I say, digging my fingers into the surface of the table. "I'm kind of out of the loop when it comes to that type of thing."

Micah shakes his head, as if to say, 'No big deal.'

Jonesy presses on. "And now you're out of a job, sweetie. Did *something happen?*"

Oh, the joys of small town living. *Something happened* when Doris Whitaker accused Philip Harlow of sexual harassment at the middle school two years before. It had been a huge scandal that had kept Jonesy's tongue limber for months.

I purse my lips. "I just realized teaching isn't for me."

"Latisha Parrish told her mother you came to this grand realization in the middle of class." She tutted me. Phyllis Jones had the nerve to tut me. "Those children need proper leadership and role models. That was just irresponsible."

"Well, so is stealing your homegirl's boyfriend right before they have major surgery, but shit happens, amIright?" I tilt my head and attempt to blind her with the wattage of my pearly whites.

Jonesy pales a fraction, then her eyes harden. "I guess some women just aren't the nurturing type. And some of us are."

Ice forms around my chest, and the healing wound in my abdomen aches.

"A classroom is a lot like a family," she says. "I would think you'd hold on tighter to the one you can still have." She places a hand on her hip, eyes glittering with pride as she watches her barbed words hit home.

Any retort I might have made sputters and dies on my lips.

"Well, I think leaving a shitty job is brave," Micah says. "You can't sell your soul for a dollar. We only get one life, you know."

Tears rim my eyes. He's talking to her, but he's looking at me.

"In fact, I think Charlotte here is my hero. Those kids will be just fine. This is a good school system, they'll find another teacher to shape those young minds in no time."

Trudy marches over, expression so placid, you'd have to have known her for a while to see the fury raging beneath the surface. I'm afraid she'll slam the two mochas in her hands down on the table. But she manages to place them gently in front of me and Micah before planting herself in Jonesy's face.

"Will you be ordering anything, *Phyllis*?" she asks, emphasizing Jonesy's hated first name. Those two have known each other longer, but I got Trudy in the split.

"Just an iced tea, thanks." Jonesy feigns obliviousness well. "It's good to see you Micah. Is Pierre here too? Maybe you two could do an impromptu performance. Our little stage is no Jimmy Kimmel, but folks here would love it. Hometown boys made good, you know?"

She's back to fluttering her eyelashes and booty tooching her ample rear. Like she doesn't have a boyfriend. My boyfriend. Whom she can keep because they deserve each other.

Micah's lips firm into a grim line. "I doubt it." Then he focuses all his attention on his coffee like the foam is the most interesting thing he's ever seen. Trudy practically drags Jonesy away, and I make a mental note to do something nice for her, like buy her a cheesecake.

We sip our drinks in companionable silence, not saying a word until the wicked witch has left the building with her iced mango tea.

"So, you're, like, a rock star?"

He grimaces. "No, I'm just the drummer in a band. Well, I was. Maybe I still am, I don't know." His voice is low and tinged with a sort of hopeless desperation I can relate to.

"You having work troubles, too?"

"Something like that." He looks up, panic in his eyes. "That's not common knowledge."

I give him a reassuring smile. "Obviously I don't have TMZ on speed dial, considering I've never heard of Riot-what?"

"RiotSphere."

"Yeah, that. Never heard of you. But I'm sure you're very talented. So, your secret is safe with me. A total stranger. Who you can completely rely on."

We laugh, and little evaporated chocolate lava molecules enter my bloodstream, because you could record his laugh and make an album of it and it would go platinum.

"Hill Valley is a small place," he says. "So I'm pretty sure I can hunt you down if I need to."

"Hunt away." Something crackles between us and I hope my

nose isn't lighting up because I didn't mean it like that. Or maybe I did. Okay, I totally did.

He has a little foam on his upper lip, and I'm about to tell him about it when his tongue peeks out and he licks it away. I stop breathing.

The bell rings again, tearing me out of the intensity of the moment. We both look away, then take sips of our drinks.

There's more ringing, coming closer, but this time it's not from the door, it's from a woman. She's young and Asian with purple platform sneakers that match her purple dreadlocks. Little bells are woven into her hair and they jingle as she approaches. Red, cat-eye glasses are perched on her nose and, from neck to knee, she's dressed like a librarian wearing an oversized, drab cardigan and brown pencil skirt.

"That's the sub," Micah whispers.

"What?"

"She's the one who gave me your purse at the school."

I look at the young woman again. She appears to be barely out of college, almost too young to substitute teach. And definitely not someone stodgy old Principal Faulkner would normally approve of. Though given the amount of notice I gave them, maybe she was the only one available.

As if she can sense us talking about her, she arrows her gaze on our table and breaks into a huge smile. Then rushes over and plants herself in the empty seat.

"Oh, good. You found each other. I'm so happy." She claps her hands together.

Micah and I look at her, then at each other.

"You're Charlotte, right? I'm Delilah." She sticks out her hand and gives me and then Micah firm handshakes. When she releases me, my palm is covered in glitter.

"Did you get stuck with my class?" I ask, wiping my hand on my khakis.

"Oh, they were totally fine. Very spirited." She nods enthusiastically setting off a chorus of chimes from the bells scattered around her person.

"That's one way to put it," I say.

"And here, something else that belongs to you." Delilah produces a notebook, from where I can't say exactly since she doesn't have a bag with her. But when I get a look at it, I snatch it out of her hands and flip through it.

"Where did you get this?" It's one of my journals. I've never taken them to school, they're way too personal, filled with my scribblings, thoughts, and poetry. "This wasn't in the drawer."

She taps her finger on her chin like she's trying to remember. Then shrugs. "I dunno. It must have been."

"No, it definitely wasn't."

Delilah leans in conspiratorially. "Well, it's not like I broke into your house while you weren't home to get it or anything." She winks, and I'm pretty sure glitter falls from her eyelashes.

This isn't my most recent notebook, it's the last one—the one I finished after I got home from the hospital. I flip through the pages, remembering those weeks of pain and the dark places my mind had gone.

A few sheets of paper fall to the ground, and Micah stoops down to pick them up. Even though the whole point of a notebook is for all the pages to be kept together, I still find myself scribbling on scraps, paper bags, receipts, or wrappers and then stuffing them inside the covers of my journal later.

Micah pats the edges of the loose pages, making a neat pile before handing them back to me. I stuff them back into the book and when I look up, Delilah is gone. No goodbyes, and no bells —it's like she just vanished.

Micah and I share a look that at least assures me I'm not the only crazy one. It occurs to me that maybe I should take a peek inside my purse to make sure nothing is missing. I have a good feeling about Micah, but this Delilah chick is another story. I'm not even sure she's a good choice to substitute teach.

"Everything there?" Micah asks, a wry look on his face.

"Yeah, I think so. It's not you I don't trust."

"No, I understand." He grins. "So, are you a poet?"

I regard him warily. He couldn't have seen much in the few seconds it took to pick up those sheets of paper. I have no idea what's even on them. "That would be stretching things a bit far. I mean, I do write poems, but I don't think that makes me a poet."

"What does it make you?"

"A girl?"

He drains the rest of his mocha. "Well, it seems like you have some skills there."

"Oh God, please tell me you didn't read anything."

"Not much, but I caught a few lines that were impressive. 'And through the brush, these tangled wilds we snake along. Our bellies raw from rubbing tracks across the ashen ground.' "

I shift uncomfortably in my seat. "You have a pretty good memory."

"Yeah, sometimes too good." His eyes take on a faraway quality for a moment before he focuses in on me. "You ever do anything with it?"

"With what? My writing? No. Definitely not." I shake my head several times for emphasis. "Teaching English doesn't even count. I just…like to get my thoughts down on paper. It calms me, helps organize my brain."

Micah slides his mug to the side and rests his forearms on the table, leaning toward me. Instinctively, I lean in as well, drawn to him like velcro.

"Have you heard of the Children's International Refugee Project?" he asks.

"Sure, they have billboards up and down the 101." Two months ago, a boat full of children had sunk off the coast of Jamaica, fleeing a brutal civil war that had spilled over into two different Central American countries.

"My mom's on the board of directors," Micah says. "They're producing this charity album as a fundraiser for this latest refugee crisis. They've already signed on a ton of big names to sing covers, but they want a few original songs. RiotSphere had a track go viral and we've been getting a lot of attention, so they asked me. That's kind of the other reason why I'm home. I have to finish this song, and it's due this weekend. They're rushing the album out and want some songs performed at the charity's big gala next week."

I'm hanging onto his words, perfectly willing to have him read the dictionary if it means I can keep listening to his voice. But I'm not connecting the dots.

He flashes that wickedly tempting smile, and I melt. "I think you could help me."

I blink. "Help you what?"

"Finish the song."

My spine straightens. Such a shame someone so beautiful is absolutely insane. "I—I don't…. I'm not—"

"Listen, I don't believe in coincidences. And my life has taught me to seize opportunities when they appear. You appeared—a woman with extra time on her hands and a gift for language that I just don't have. I need help, and I think fate intervened to bring you to me in my time of need."

I heard only a few words from that sentence, mainly: *I, need* and *you*. Stars light up my eyes until my brain puts her foot down. "I've never written a song before, Micah. And I'm flattered you think I can do this, but I just don't think it's possible."

He sits back in his chair, gaze never leaving my face. I start to heat under his perusal. "You know how we got that Jimmy Kimmel gig?"

I shake my head.

"A song I co-wrote with my band member Pierre made its way into a meme. The Grocery Cart Towing Challenge. Kids film themselves sitting in a grocery cart holding on to the side of a moving car and driving down the highway. For some reason, our song plays in the background. So far eight teens have been hospitalized."

"Geez, that's awful. I'm so sorry." I'm pretty sure at least a few of my students—former students—would be intrigued by something so stupid and dangerous.

"I never thought something I created would get used like that. It kind of broke me."

"To the point where you're not sure you want to be in the band anymore?"

"Yeah. I figured, this charity album is a small way to make up for it. A way to create something in the world—to leave a positive mark instead. If I'm remembered at all, I don't want it to be as the guy who created the song a bunch of kids broke their backs to."

Understanding flows through me. "You want to leave a legacy."

"Exactly. And this charity album seems like a good start. I've just never been a lyrics guy. That was Pierre's deal. And he's not on board with giving a song away for free." Pain and anger lace his voice. "I need someone to help."

"But why me?"

He smiles. "I have a good feeling about you, Charlotte. And I trust my gut."

My eyes must be shooting out warning lasers because he holds his hands up in surrender. "Okay, okay, tell you what? How about you just agree to be my muse? You don't have to do anything but show up. I'll write the song and you just..." He waves his arm around.

"Sit there and look pretty?"

"Yeah. Something like that."

His grin disarms me—like, I can't feel my arms right now—and his chuckle rearranges something inside my chest. "I don't know..."

"Do it for the children, Charlotte. You kind of owe them."

It's wild. Completely crazy. But is it any crazier than quitting your job in the middle of the day? Walking out on a full class-room of juvenile delinquents? I really need to start looking for a new way to feed myself and pay for my apartment and my hair products, but his song is due this weekend.

"Okay," I say.

And because the gods are kind and benevolent, Micah reaches over the table to grab my hands in his and squeezes them. I nearly come off my seat at the contact. A circuit in my chest shorts.

I can always start job hunting next week.

FOUR

WE AGREE to meet at his place, or rather, his mother's place, where he's staying. Since he's been on tour for the past few years, virtually non-stop, he doesn't actually keep an apartment.

Google Maps takes me to a nice neighborhood on a hill that looks over the Bay. There's even a little turnout where you can park and look down on the Golden Gate Bridge and the city of San Francisco just across the water. It reminds me of how much I like living here in the tiny, garden apartment that I can just barely afford on a teacher's salary. Without a job it will be impossible.

I turn into the driveway of an enormous two-story Craftsman in the well-heeled neighborhood and park behind a Mini Cooper out of which—no lie—five clowns come out. I do a double take to make sure I'm not imagining it. Then I take out my camera. Pics or it didn't happen, as the kids say.

One of the clowns stubs out a cigarette on the ground with a giant orange shoe before entering the house. The front door is open, so I follow behind them, trying to keep my jaw in place. More clowns fill the entryway. There are clowns in the dining room, the kitchen, and on the steps.

Micah appears from down the center hall, and I maneuver through greasepaint and fluorescent wigs and polka dots to get to him.

"Care to explain?" I ask, motioning to the circus surrounding us.

"My mom is auditioning talent for my brother's birthday party."

"Of course she is."

"Come on, it's quiet downstairs."

He leads me to the finished basement, which is indeed quiet. A little kid sits on the giant sectional playing a video game.

"Charlotte this is my brother Jude, Jude this is Charlotte."

Micah's brother is brown-skinned with a laser cut high top fade. He's no older than seven and looks nothing like Micah.

He glances up at me while his fingers move faster than light-speed on the video game controller. "Made it through the clowns, huh?" he says.

I like this kid.

I try to think of something to say that's not an insult. "Your mom has an impressive attention to detail."

Jude snorts. "You could say that again."

"Um, do you even like clowns?"

He shrugs. "Does it matter?" This is a kid resigned to the state of the world. I'm not sure if that's especially prescient or just sad. He goes back to his game—some sort of first person shooter, except the gun in the foreground shoots giant exploding globs of paint. Or something.

"Come on," Micah says, picking up an acoustic guitar and leading me to a door in the back. It's a comfortable guest bedroom painted a dark beige with beige carpeting and a beige bedspread. There's an armchair in the corner and a laptop and notebook spread out on the queen-sized bed. I sit in the armchair, and Micah settles on the bed.

"So, what exactly does a muse do?" I feel a little nervous, but he looks perfectly comfortable. Today, he's got on a black, V-neck t-shirt and artfully shredded jeans. I feel slovenly in leggings and a slouchy T-shirt, but I wanted to keep it casual.

"Just observe. Send out inspiring creative energy, that sort of thing."

"Okay." I clasp my hands as he begins strumming the guitar. He plays a melody, a little plaintive but with a bluesy edge.

I streamed RiotSphere's first album the evening I met him. Their sound is not what I expected. It's old school rhythm and blues-style rock with hip-hop sensibilities. I'm not a huge fan of the song that went viral, "Jesus's Cup Holder," but the other stuff on their album sank into my head and stayed there.

The tune he's playing sounds great, and I begin humming along. Micah stops every so often to change a chord. He's apparently recording parts of the song on his computer as well. It's fascinating to watch him work, even though I'm pretty sure he doesn't need me for anything.

Then he starts to sing. "Kids, kids, everywhere, in the water, in the air / Walking somewhere really far, cause they don't have a car."

He nods like he's just come up with something that doesn't sound insipid, meanwhile his expression is completely serious. He scribbles a few words in a notebook, then goes back to his strumming. I look around to make sure a hidden camera isn't behind me.

"Everybody old or young, needs a place to lay their head / Some will find a cardboard box, some will find a bed."

I think what he's writing down are these actual words. On paper. Like he means to save them and, I don't know, repeat them to another human being.

"Micah."

"Hmm?" He crosses something out then rewrites it.

"Come on. Seriously?"

He looks up, guileless. "What? I told you lyrics aren't my thing."

I shake my head. "Your reverse psychology tricks are so, so sad. I can't believe you would stoop so low."

The innocent expression on his face doesn't fool me. This man is messing with me, and I know it.

"No, your presence is helping, I'm feeling more creative already." He grins. And then he starts singing again.

"A box is not that comfortable, it's better than a stone / And if you're really that tired, a board's better than none." He pronounces 'none' so it rhymes with 'stone' and I can't really handle anything else.

"All right buddy, I'm going to have to stop you there. You are not only mangling the English language, I'm pretty sure you're ruining several others as well. What is this song about?"

"Well, I want it to really tug at your heartstrings, like that Sarah McLachlan song in those puppy commercials."

"Everyone knows those commercials are really a Turing test to weed out sophisticated Artificial Intelligence from real people."

"If you're not crying by the end, you're obviously a bot planning the destruction of humanity," Micah deadpans.

"Exactly." I lean forward in my chair. "But I thought this charity was for Children's International Refugee Project."

"It is."

"Isn't their acronym, CHIRP?"

"Yeah, and?"

"So maybe the music should be a little more upbeat?" I say. "What if you increase the tempo so it isn't so dirge-like?"

He frowns. "It's not dirge-like."

"It's definitely dirge-adjacent."

His fingers go into position on the guitar and he begins playing, speeding up the melody this time. I pat my thigh in time with the beat and an image pops into my head.

This is how I usually write poems. Something flashes in my mind—usually a fully formed visual that makes me feel a very specific way and then I have to write. I was so determined not to help him in this scheme though, I didn't even bring a notebook with me, so I leap for the bed, grab his and shuffle for a clean page.

I write, ignoring the satisfied smile spreading across Micah's ridiculously handsome face.

FIVE

"OKAY, so how about this: 'How long will we look away? The silence it drowns us. If we don't stand up today, tomorrow is groundless.'?"

Micah plays the melody he's still tweaking and sings what I've written. His voice is scratchy and deep. He's not the lead singer of RiotSphere, but he could be. Watching him strum the guitar strings, scribble notations, and fiddle with his laptop, I know he's the real deal. A true talent. It makes me feel even more like a fraud.

"So we have the ongoing metaphor about the ocean and water—"

"That's why you added 'groundless.' " He bobs his head up and down. "I get it. Very clever."

I blush, trying not to let the compliment sink in.

"Maybe that could be the bridge." He plays it again as the bridge of the song and it sounds perfect. It really does seem to be turning into the anthem he wanted. One that will hopefully make people care about the refugee children who have lost their parents to violence and war almost as much as they care about puppies. I want the words to match Micah's music and take root in a part of the listener's soul—I just don't know if I can pull it off. In fact, I'm sure I can't.

"Is this really working?" I ask, rising from my seat on the floor. I usually move around a lot when writing, and I'd already sat on every surface in the room and several spots on the carpet.

"Yeah, it's great. We're nearly there."

I shake my head, unsure. Micah looks at me, focusing his intensity in a way that makes me start to sweat from the heat pouring off of him. I've been able to focus on the work and the words, caught up in the act of creation, but in the lulls, this crackling attraction for him takes over and makes my brain overheat.

"What?" I ask, fanning myself with my hand.

"Let's take a break," he says. "Come on, I want you to see something."

We exit into the basement. I lost track of time while we were in Micah's room, but it's been hours. The TV down here is off, and Jude has disappeared. The house also appears blissfully clown-free. Micah takes me out the front door and we head down the sidewalk of the uncomfortably quiet neighborhood.

"Why did you become a teacher, anyway?"

I wonder if I should tell him, if it makes me seem pathetic, but I decide to go with the truth. "Everyone always told me I should. I guess I believed them."

He leads me down a paved path between the houses. We walk at a steady pace and he doesn't seem to be in a hurry.

"So what did you want to do?"

"That's just the thing, I have no idea. I'm good at taking care of people. I raised my little brother after our mom ditched us."

He looks over at me, eyebrow raised. "Did you know your dad?"

"Oh yeah, he was around, kind of. He's in the army and never met a transfer he didn't like. We lived out of boxes my whole childhood."

I stumble a little on a crack in the path, and Micah grabs my elbow to right me. Embarrassment heats my cheeks, so I just keep talking.

"One Christmas, Mom went to visit her parents in Norway and just never came back. Two moves after that, my brother Mat failed the sixth grade. At that point I just refused to move any more. So me and Mat stayed here while Dad trotted all over the globe chasing a higher rank."

"How old were you?"

"Seventeen. I put off college until Mat was situated and by the time I went, I just majored in Education because I knew I could get a job. I thought I had the temperament for it. It made sense."

"So you're mom's Norwegian and your dad's…?"

"Jamaican, originally. That thing about the work ethic is no joke, at least not for him." I snort. "The Colonel will not be happy when he finds out I quit my job." The shadow of his future wrath hangs over me and I shiver, though the October air is warm.

We emerge from the path onto the overlook I passed on the way in, and a perfect, breathtaking view of the bay and the city and the ocean beyond. We sit down on a patch of grass bathed in late afternoon sunlight.

"So if you could do anything, be anything, what would you be?" Micah asks.

I look over to find that instead of watching the incredible view in front of us, he's staring at me. My heartbeat begins to race until it's chugging along like the little engine that could. I forget his question and wrack my brain, rewinding a few seconds.

"Anything?" I ask. Honestly, after being locked in a small room with this man all day, if I could do anything I wanted, it would be him, but even in its blood-starved state my brain tells me that's not an appropriate response.

"I'd write movies." I frown, wondering who said that. It sounded like me, but I haven't thought of that wild dream in years. It's so impractical, so implausible. But for some reason, my answer makes Micah smile, and the engine in my chest shifts into a higher gear.

"Movies, cool." He nods like this makes perfect sense.

"I don't know why I said that. I mean, people don't just… write movies." I finish lamely.

"How do you think they get written?" he asks, smirking.

"I don't know, artificial intelligence?"

"You mean the ones that make it past the Sarah McLachlan Turing test?"

"They've been warning us for decades of their plan. We really shouldn't be surprised when one of them finally goes ahead and launches the nukes."

His laugh is melodic; he bumps my shoulder. I feel the contact sizzle all the way through my body.

"You can write movies. If that's what you want."

"I feel like I'd need to go back to school or get special training or something."

"I don't know. Not every screenwriter in Hollywood has a degree. I think sometimes they just," he lifts a shoulder, "start writing and see if it's good."

Start writing and see if it's good. He makes it sound so simple, like it doesn't require ultimate confidence, or rich parents, or at the very least knowing someone important.

But Micah's grin is full of confidence. "You're already a really good writer. You totally saved my song."

I bump his shoulder this time and say, "Your song was just really bad. Almost anything would have been better."

His eyes smile at me, then he sobers. "It's okay for you to be good at things." I'm not sure he's even noticed the view; the whole time we've been sitting here, his eyes haven't strayed from my face. My backbone has turned into a noodle, and I lean against him, more to hold my torso up than for any other reason.

"I'd love to be good at things," I tell him. "I just wish it was as easy as you seem to think it is."

"Oh, I know it's not easy, trust me. But it's not impossible. People do it. You'd probably have to work your ass off and try your best to be in the right places at the right times and network with the right people. But you can do it. There are thousands of screenwriters working today. You could be one of them. If you want." His eyes bore into me like a glittering, diamond-tipped drill. "It's okay to get what you want."

The moment hangs there, encasing his words like glass. His eyes dart to my lips and we're so close. I'm leaning against him, but I didn't realize how little distance there was between us until the bottom drops out of my stomach. I can't breathe or think or anything, I just watch as he erases the few inches between us.

But it's taking too gosh-dang long, and so I meet him halfway.

His lips are warm and full, and he tastes like oranges. No, orangesicle, the subtle difference making itself abundantly clear when his tongue breaches my mouth. He's gentle but demanding. His grip on my waist grows tight.

Large, warm hands skim up my back, and I'm not sure if I'm still upright or have fallen into a gravity pit because I can't feel the ground below me anymore. I'm conscious of pressing my hand to his cheek, feeling his stubble abrade my palm as I drink him in.

Both of his hands move back down to encircle my waist now, holding me like a vise, like he's afraid I'm going to go somewhere. What I should tell him is I'm never going anywhere, not while what we're doing right now is an option. The kiss grows all consuming. I feel off-balance and my lungs need air, but I don't pull back. Not yet. Not until I absolutely have to, and then he's staring at me and the sun has somehow set.

Darkness surrounds us and the kaleidoscope of lights across

the Bay makes him look magical. This whole experience of meeting him has been magical.

The honk of a foghorn somewhere on the water vibrates through me, convincing me this isn't just a dream. He's real, but I still feel a little fantastical.

Micah grins.

"What?" I whisper.

"Here's to getting what you want," he says and kisses me again.

SIX

IT'S BEEN a long time since I've been at an eight-year-old's birthday party. My brother Mat's would have been the last one, I guess, and I'm pretty sure that Dad was at work and Mom bought cupcakes from the grocery store and stuck some candles in one of them.

She wasn't super into the whole maternal thing—at least, not with us. I wonder if things are different with her new family. With the younger half-brother and sister I've never met over in Norway.

The front pathway to Micah's mother's house is bordered in two giant, free-standing balloon sculptures. You can probably hear the voices of laughing, screaming children all the way in Sausalito. I wonder if the neighbors mind, but as I enter the house I realize that the entire neighborhood must be here.

It's a big house, but it's absolutely packed with people. Adult people are the only ones I see as I wade through them, trying to make my way down to the basement where I'm supposed to meet Micah.

I peek through into the kitchen and the backyard beyond. What looks like an entire amusement park has been set up back there. I think I actually see roller coaster tracks, but a wall of bodies quickly blocks my view.

I bump into a few people before I make it to the basement steps. The party continues downstairs, but I'm able to squeeze into Micah's bedroom, half afraid it will be overflowing like the rest of the house.

Fortunately, he's here alone, guitar in hand and headphones on. He grins when I push my way inside and shut the door, leaning against it, breath shaky.

He stands to greet me and before I can get my heartbeat back to normal from the *American Ninja Warrior*-style obstacle course I've just traversed, his arms are around me and I'm sinking into his kiss.

I had almost made myself believe it wasn't real. The mouth-watering scent of him, the way his arms crush me like he never wants to let go. Breathing is for suckers anyway, I'd rather inhale Micah exclusively. I would if he'd let me.

When we break apart, he's looking at me with heavy-lidded eyes. A crash sounds overhead, and the corner of his mouth curls up. "Hi."

"Hi, yourself," I reply. I pull away from him to gather what's left of my composure. "Are you ready?"

He's still looking at me like he wants to treat me like an ice cream cone. I shiver and try to redirect him—I'm not against becoming his personal dessert, but not with the fire hazard going on in this house right now and an army of seven and eight-year-olds on the other side of the basement window.

Swallowing, I cross to the other side of the room, putting some space between us. "Are you sure you want to play the song for them? This may not be the ideal venue."

"Jude is into the idea. Plus, the song's for a kid's charity, what better way to make sure we've got it right than to test it out in front of a bunch of kids?"

Screams of delight peal, seeming to tunnel through the

concrete foundation of the house. "I'm not so sure we'll have a captive audience," I say.

"Hey, if the song can pull their attention away from the rides and the games and the candy, then we know it's good."

"Yeah, and don't forget the clowns."

"Oh, there aren't any clowns."

"What?"

He shrugs. "Mom decided she didn't want any after all." He picks up his guitar, leaning towards me, but I scurry out of the way. He just chuckles and leads me back into the melee.

SEVEN

THE DJ TURNS down the hip-hop music that had been blasting, masking some of the sounds of the games and rides that fill every corner of the massive back yard. Micah stands on the narrow stage, in front of the turntables, fiddling with the neck of his guitar. I'm off to the side, at the edge of the stage, the only one present really paying attention to him.

That is until the microphone feeds back. I wince and cover my ears as the high-pitched whine goes on and on. One look at his face confirms my suspicion that he's doing this on purpose.

When he moves the mic away from the speaker, the entire yard is quiet. "Happy birthday, Jude! In honor of my little homie's special day, I wanted to see what you thought about this song. It's called, 'Going Under,' and I had a very special lady help me out with the lyrics."

When he looks over at me, I want to sink into the ground, but my heart melts just a little bit as well. His long fingers strum the strings, and he begins to sing the song we wrote together.

I'm convinced that at any moment the noise of the games will start up again, the bright, bubbly sounds like melted lollipops poured into your ears. Or that the kids will start shouting and screaming, running around and ignoring what's going on up on the stage in favor of their normal funtime pursuits.

But when I dare look around, they're all rapt. Focused completely on what's happening on stage. That's when I notice that almost all of these kids are wearing variations of the same t-shirt, just in different colors. The CHIRP logo is emblazoned on the front. These kids are refugees from the charity. This song is actually about them.

I get a little misty-eyed hearing Micah's smooth voice sing my lyrics. And the tears really start to fall when I see the children hanging onto every word. After the third chorus, some are even singing along. I've never had something I've done creatively be heard by this many people before. It's enough to truly humble me.

When the last chords play, there's silence for an endless moment.

And then the applause begins.

Adults crowd around the sides of the yard and peer out of windows and doors in the house, all cheering. Kids are jumping up and down, clapping and screaming. So this is what it's like to be a rock star. Micah seems to take it all in stride. He thanks them, wishes his brother a happy birthday again, and then jumps off the stage. Where he's promptly mobbed by a gang of very intent, very focused, miniature humans.

They're all talking at the same time, some are speaking different languages, no one seems to want anything other than to be heard. Some attach themselves to his legs, there's a chorus of voices demanding that he play the song again and before too long, he does. The kids eat it up the second time, and afterwards I actually lose Micah in the sea of tiny heads. My chest is completely hollow. I'm pretty sure I'm in love.

An hour later, the party has resumed. Micah has managed to tear himself away from his new pint-sized fan club. A trio of adult women march toward him with a disturbing amount of intensity. I sense "Biggest Fan" vibes coming from them as they pass the bouncy house. Micah grabs my hand and tugs.

"Come on," he whispers, and we make a run for it.

There aren't many places to go since the yard is now a theme park, but soon enough we're crouching behind the pool house, hiding from all the attention.

"Those kids really loved you," I tell him. The adults seemed to as well, but I don't mention that.

"They're great. They've had a hard time, but they're good. No child should have to live like that."

"Yeah that's true. Are you satisfied that the song is up to snuff?"

"It's okay. The lyrics are fantastic at least." He grins. "I'm going to send our temp track to the producer tonight and they'll be recording it on Monday."

"So fast? That's amazing." I hear footsteps and hope that no one finds our little hiding spot at least for a few more minutes. "So you're going to the big gala next week?"

Am I angling for an invitation? Maybe. But I think I'm being subtle about it.

Micah's sunny expression darkens a little. "Pierre is asking about me going back on tour with him. They're leaving on Thursday."

My heart sinks. "Oh." Maybe now that he's done his part for the charity he'll feel like he's made up for all those kids who got hurt.

"I don't know if I'm going or not. I'm still not sure what my future is in RiotSphere."

He takes my hand and holds it in his, then brings it up to his lips and kisses it. My chest flutters, and I'm almost incapable of coherent thought. "Y—you don't want to be a rock star anymore?"

"It's not as glamorous as it seems. We've been touring for the past six years, almost nonstop. It's the only way to make a living. I'm thinking maybe I need to settle down a little more. You know, put down some roots."

"Oh, really? All of this looks appealing to you, does it?" I wave my hand around the cacophony of children screaming around our hiding place.

"All of this wouldn't be the worst thing in the world." His gaze holds on me and it feels significant.

I freeze, and the little glow inside me fades. "Um, well yeah, I could see that. You'll probably make a terrific dad one day."

He must see the change in me. "I mean, not at this moment you know, but maybe…. What's wrong, Char?"

"Nothing. Nothing. I'm glad I could help you with the song. I think it'll be great. Thank you for giving me this opportunity."

He's looking at me like I'm rambling like a crazy person, which I guess I am. But the moment is over, and I have to get out of here. "I guess I'll see you around. I'd better go." I stand and start dusting off my sundress, straightening imaginary wrinkles.

"Charlotte, wait, what's going on?"

"Nothing, I just need to get home. Start job hunting you know? These curls don't de-frizz themselves. And my haircare product bills alone require a good twenty percent of my income." I laugh, high-pitched and fake and make a beeline through a narrow path I've spotted that leads away from the house. Micah jogs after me.

"Charlotte!"

"I wish you the best Micah," I say over my shoulder as I speed-walk. "I really do. I think you're amazing, and I hope you find a way to leave your legacy."

And then I'm at the gate, fumbling with it through the tears building in my eyes. I lift the latch and race through before he can stop me.

EIGHT

DELILAH MATERIALIZES in the alley behind Coffee Bar and shakes out her dreadlocks. In the dying, golden sunlight they look almost brown. She shudders.

Today she's dressed in what she hopes is a professional outfit. There's no dress code for the Cupid Guild, each agent is left on their own to decide what's best. And professional for Delilah means a sparkly purple tank top, pleated miniskirt, and her knee-high platform boots.

Dress to impress, her matriarch always says. Her assignment has been a tricky one, and she's got to make sure it goes through. Managing the love lives of humans is serious business.

She waves a hand to unlock the deadbolt on the back door of the coffee shop and walks through the back hall, the pretty bells strung through her hair singing the song of her arrival. According to the ping she'd received on her trans-dimensional tablet, one half of her assignment should be seated at the bar, talking to her best friend Trudy, and drowning her sorrows in caffeine.

As she approaches, Trudy turns to stare at Delilah, her jaw dropping open. "Where did you come from?"

Delilah waves cheerily. "Good afternoon. Or is it already good evening? I'm never sure where the cut-off point between afternoon and evening is? How does anyone know which one to say?"

She waits for an answer, but both women just stare at her like she's got something growing out of her head. She's pretty sure she's wearing an entirely human form right now—she double-checked before materializing, but she's gotten it wrong before. She bends to inspect herself in the shiny surface of the espresso machine.

Yup, all human. She turns back to the women.

"I'm calling the police," Trudy says.

Delilah looks around, shocked. "Why? Is someone hurt? Did something get stolen?"

"Who. The hell. Are you?"

"That's Delilah," Charlotte answers. "The sub." She tilts her head to the side and squints. "Or, maybe not."

"I *am* Delilah," she says, sticking out her hand. Trudy doesn't shake it. Delilah frowns. She's sure that's rude. She rounds the bar and takes the seat next to Charlotte. "You're upset about Micah."

Charlotte's eyes are red. Two large, empty mugs sit in front of her, already consumed, while another one rests between her palms.

"You're not going to sleep at all tonight, again, with all that caffeine in your system," Delilah admonishes. "You're very sensitive to it, you know."

The two friends look at each other and then back to Delilah, who rewinds the conversation in her head to make sure she had been speaking the correct language. Human tongues are all so similar, with their limited range of sounds and funny way words leave their mouths. She's pretty sure she'd been speaking English.

"The gala is on Friday, and you don't want bags under your eyes, right? Sleep really is very important."

Charlotte's hand rushes to her face to touch the dark skin under her eyes as if to check for bags.

Trudy finally unhinges her jaw and clamps her mouth shut. Her phone is in her hand, but she hasn't dialed the police yet. "How do you know about the gala?"

Delilah waves a hand. Anyone who was anyone knew about the gala. "So what do you have left to decide on? Hair? Nails? I know you *must* have your dress picked out."

Charlotte sniffs and shakes her head. "I haven't thought about any of those things because I'm not going to the gala."

Delilah scratches her ear to make sure she's heard right. "Did you say you weren't going?"

"Right."

"But why not?"

Charlotte throws her hands up in frustration or desperation or some sort of *-ation*. "Because I'm a mess. Because I ran away from him before he could ask me. Because he's not the right one for me. No one's the right one for me."

"No, I assure you, he is." Delilah pulls out her tablet and taps on it to bring up their file. "See, you two were evaluated based on 1.5 billion data sets. You're a 98% match."

Trudy squints at the screen of the tablet and frowns. "There's nothing but a video of jellybeans pouring into a jar on there."

Delilah looks down. "Well, yes, that's how it appears to you, because 1.5 billion data sets are impossible for the human brain to comprehend. But trust me, the match is cosmically sound."

"*Cosmically* sound?"

"Yes." Delilah nods enthusiastically. "What's really the problem, sweetie?" She pats Charlotte's hand.

"I'm just feeling like...like not a whole person. Like I can't give him everything he wants, you know? I just—" She shakes her head, moving her hand to her stomach, unconsciously. "I just don't think it will work out."

"Well, shouldn't he get a say?" Delilah asks. Charlotte's head shoots up. "You're worried about children and you think he'll act like Tanner did and leave at the first hint of trouble."

Trudy slaps the counter. "This is what I've been telling her."

"Well, Tanner was a douche knapsack," Delilah says. "Is Micah a douche knapsack?"

Charlotte's wide eyes are round. She shakes her head.

"Of course not. 1.5 billion data points wouldn't match you with someone so shallow, and a cheater besides. If you're really worried about Micah's reaction, why don't you just tell him and see what he says?"

The expression on Charlotte's face makes it clear she hadn't even considered that. "So, I should just tell him?"

Delilah smiles encouragingly. Trudy's eyes widen, staring over both their shoulders.

"Tell me what?" a deep voice says from behind them.

Right on time, Delilah thinks, and snaps her fingers, disappearing.

NINE

I SWIVEL AROUND in my seat slowly, my cheeks on fire. They're probably as red as my nose and my eyes. Of course the first time I see Micah after running away from him this afternoon and dodging all his texts and calls, I look like something the cat dragged in.

But when I meet his eyes, they don't recoil, and he doesn't look mad. Hurt maybe, pained, but not angry.

"Tell me what, Charlotte?" I hear footsteps retreating. I'm guessing that Trudy and the woman, who I can only assume is my fairy godmother, have decided to give me and Micah some privacy. Since he first spoke, it's like no one else in the world exists but him.

He tracked me down here, and I owe him an apology. "I'm sorry for bailing on you like that earlier. I just—"

"Listen, I'm sorry if I was moving too fast with the talk of futures and kids and stuff. I promise I'm not some creep who fell in love with you at first sight and mapped out our futures in that very moment." He smiles a weird, tense smile.

My mouth moves for a second before being able to form

audible words. "In the future you haven't mapped out, you want kids?"

He searches my face. "I don't know. Maybe."

"Because I can't. Have kids." I motion towards my abdomen. "It was all messed up in there, so they had to take some things out." I fidget with my fingers. "I'm actually still recovering from the surgery."

Understanding dawns in his eyes. I brace myself for his retreat. For a cold glaze to fall across him now that he knows the fulness of my limitations. But instead of pulling away, he steps closer. "Is that why you left? Being around the kids...was it painful?"

I shake my head. "No, not exactly. I just— There's a door that's closed now. It used to be open, but now it's shut. And that made me look at my life and everything and just wonder, what am I doing? How am I living?"

I stand up and take a breath. Grab his hands in mine because I need this connection with him, even if it won't last. "You said you want a legacy. I've heard that before. My ex wanted that too, and he found it with someone else. My life isn't turning out how I expected and it's just— I don't want to bring someone else down with me."

He's quiet for a while, his gaze on our clasped hands. I try to pull away, but he squeezes tighter.

He clears his throat. "I was five when I was adopted. Jude was a newborn when my parents got him. We were both born to drug addicted mothers. So it's true, some doors are closed for you right now, but there are plenty of windows. If you want a family, you can have one."

My throat is thick with emotion.

"Listen, it's not like I have my shit together. I live on a bus. I don't even have an apartment anymore. I'm a thirty-five-year-old man living in his mother's basement. I'm not in a position to judge."

I lift a shoulder. "Yeah, but you've been on Jimmy Kimmel."

He laughs a chocolate lava sound that fills up all the empty spaces inside me. "Charlotte Woodson, would you like to go on a date with me? I hear there's some fancy gala happening next week."

I stand up straighter and look him in the eye. "Do we have to wait until next week?"

And then he wraps me tight in his embrace and kisses me until I see stars.

EPILOGUE

MICAH and I move slowly across the dance floor, the only satellites in an orbit of our own. His hands wrap possessively around my waist and I don't know how much longer we'll be staying at this little shindig. At least until the performance part of the gala is over and our song is sung by a rising pop star who recorded it earlier this week for the charity album.

But right now, it's just us, lost in the soft music and the magic I feel when he touches me. Then a tap at my shoulder has me pulling away from my happy place and staring into a face framed by purple dreadlocks.

"You were right," I tell Delilah, my voice dreamy. "You and your data points."

She gives a little wave. "Hi, Micah. Of course I was. That was never in doubt. But I have someone else I want you to meet. He's in the bathroom now because I spilled cocktail sauce all over his tux, but it'll come right out." She puts a finger to her chin. "Or else I'll have to emergency requisition him a new shirt."

Micah's eyebrows rise, but he wisely stays silent. I think it's probably best not to pay too close attention to all the things I don't understand in what she says. "I hope this isn't another match, because I'm perfectly happy with the one I've got." Micah squeezes me tighter.

Delilah's smile brightens a few watts. "Oh no, he's your new boss. He's looking for an assistant. Wants help managing his schedule, transcribing meetings, some light copyediting."

A fairy godmother who also helps with job searching, interesting. "Oh, well, thanks Delilah. That was awfully nice of you. But I'm not sure if that's—"

"I also think he said something about dusting off his awards case. Apparently, he's got a shelf full of screenwriting awards. No need to rub it in our faces, am I right? I'll point him out to you when he gets back from the loo."

Little bells echo as she spins around and heads off the dance floor.

Micah gives me a look that's somewhere between shell-shocked (a reaction I'm pretty sure Delilah receives often) and proud. I tuck my head back against his chest and keep dancing.

I could really get used to this whole 'getting what you want' thing.

THE CUPID FIASCO

BOOK 4

While trapped in a basement during an earthquake, sparks fly between co-workers Luce and Mat—too bad they're sparks of rage. So when Mat needs a fake girlfriend for a weekend engagement party in wine country, there's no way Luce will say yes… is there?

It's up to the Cupid Guild to show this salty pair how sweet it could be.

A sexy, standalone romance with a paranormal touch. This novella first appeared in *Heart's Kiss* magazine, under the title "Before I Break."

ONE

LUCE SPUN in the swivel chair, her sensible heels lightly skimming the linoleum. The lunch rush rioted around her in a pastel blur. She embraced the dizziness—she felt more in control knowing she could simply plant her feet on the ground and the world would right itself. Few things in life were that simple.

A small, static figure set apart from the whirling din caused her to skid to a stop. The little boy, four or five years old, whose mouth and cheeks were smudged with what she suspected was cherry chocolate from Delilah's Candy Bar just across the courtyard, stood staring at Luce. She rolled her chair closer and leaned down.

"Do you need help?"

He blinked a few times and licked at the chocolate still coating his lips.

"It seems this little guy is lost," a voice rumbled from above.

She shifted her gaze to the right and encountered a pair of scuffed black boots. Directly above them were sturdy canvas pants, a plaid button-up shirt, and the pièce de résistance—Mathias Woodson's movie star–worthy face, the corners of his mouth turned up in a smile.

Great.

She stood, though even in her professional, patent leather, slightly squishy heels, she was no match for his height. Still, she straightened her pencil skirt and cleared her throat. *Close your mouth, remember to breathe, blink, and for God's sake don't stare.*

After two months of working with him, she still had to run through the checklist every time she encountered the man. She refused to be like the gaggle of women trailing after him, drooling at his feet.

Though she'd checked off all the most likely areas of possible embarrassment, she could only hold his gaze for a moment before retreating to the safety of considering the little boy. "What's your name, sweetheart?"

A blank stare was the only response. She shot a questioning glance to Mat, who shrugged. "I think he took the whole 'don't talk to strangers' thing to heart."

"Superb."

The little boy was adorable—dark curly hair, sun-toasted bronze skin. In fact, he and Mat could have been brothers, or father and son, they looked so much alike. Luce scanned the area for desperate parents searching for their missing child.

Lost kids were part of the territory when manning the information booth at the Button Factory. The shopping center-slash-tourist trap at Fisherman's Wharf in San Francisco had been an actual button-producing factory up until the mid-1960s. After a few decades of neglect, the building was reno-vated and repurposed and now featured three levels of shop-ping and dining. Tourists from all over the world packed the brick building, and the first floor info booth was at the center of it all.

Luce had first gotten the job in college when she'd been a hospitality major. She liked people and loved talking to travelers from the countries she'd always dreamed of visiting. Though she'd eventually changed her major to public relations and gotten promoted after graduation to work in the Factory's business office on the fourth floor, she looked forward to days like today when she was asked to fill in for an absent co-worker.

With another look at the cherubic, chocolate-covered face, Luce picked up the intercom and called the security office to put their guards on alert for the parents. When she hung up, Mat was kneeling down, wiping the boy's mouth with a wet nap he'd produced from somewhere.

The boy, fairly stoic up until then, looked around with a freshly clean face and burst into tears. Mat's eyes widened. He turned to Luce, silently pleading for help with the bawling child. She sighed and sat back in her chair, then lifted the boy into her lap.

"Your mommy and daddy will be here soon. I bet they're looking everywhere for you right now." As she tried to encourage him, a cold fear sliced her belly. She hoped her words weren't lies. All parents were not created equal, as she well knew.

She spun him around in the chair a few times, racking her brain for something to calm him down. His T-shirt featured a colorful image of the caboose of a train.

"Do you like trains?"

He sniffed a few times before nodding.

"Have you ever been on a real train before?"

He shook his head.

"Neither have I, unless you count BART—that's the subway —but I don't. One day I'm going to take a train trip and sit right up front near the engine. Wouldn't that be fun?"

The boy cracked a smile. "Thomas is a train engine."

"You're right!"

Mat squatted down. "I've been on lots of trains and they are really fun. I took a train in India that had goats and chickens walking down the aisles."

The kid's eyes widened and Mat nodded.

"The smell was terrible."

Mat held his nose, and the boy broke out into an infectious

round of giggles. Luce couldn't help but smile, though she dropped it when Mat winked at her. He then launched into a tale that involved a goat, his favorite T-shirt, and a tug of war that didn't end well.

Those definitely were not her ovaries brawling inside of her, vying for first crack at this delightful specimen of man. She clenched her belly and willed her ladybits to calm the hell down. There really wasn't anything to get excited about.

When she looked up, Randy, one of the security guards, was approaching ahead of a rather calm looking man and woman, both impeccably dressed.

"Freddy," said an exasperated, statuesque blonde with an expensive-looking haircut. "You're going to make us miss our bus to Napa. Do you know how expensive those tickets were?" She spoke with a European accent Luce couldn't place.

The father, a short, roly poly man with skin a shade darker than Luce's own ebony complexion, spoke in a heavy Jamaican accent. "Dat boy don't have da sense he was born with. And look, him run off wit da candy and ate it all!"

As she stood, settling Freddy to his feet, Luce schooled her features, masking her anger. Suddenly she was seven years old again, swinging her legs on the metal chair of a hotel's security office, pretending to watch the cartoons on the television the kind guards had set her in front of. Hours later, when her parents finally returned for her, they'd chastised *her* for making them miss their bus and resulting in a change fee for new tickets. Was it too much to ask that your own parents not check out and leave their daughter behind?

Her eyes stung as tears threatened from the long-buried memory. She clenched her jaw, looked away and held her breath. Counted to ten. She'd been in the service industry long enough to know how to keep from strangling the customers.

When she'd regained her composure and looked up, Mat was peering at her. Luce plastered on a professionally plastic smile.

Randy went through the procedures to ensure that these in fact were the parents and not some strange kidnappers, but the boy's joy at seeing the couple was obvious, even as they berated him.

"I expect you to behave, Freddy. You know we could have taken this trip by ourselves and not had half of the hassles. I told you—"

"First time in San Francisco?" Luce asked, rocking slightly on the balls of her feet.

The woman looked up mid-diatribe, as if surprised to see Luce standing there. "Yes, I've always wanted to come, but Vernon has very little time off." She patted her husband's arm, but his attention was firmly on the window display of Delilah's Candy Bar across the way.

"I'm glad you could make the trip. There's so much to see. And where are you from?"

"Norway, originally. But we've been in London for the past few years."

"Oh really? My mother's from Norway," Mat said. The woman raised her eyebrows and ran her eyes down his body. Slowly. Her thorough scan was both skeptical and lascivious. Luce bristled.

A string of foreign words flowed from Mat's mouth. If that was Norwegian, it sounded like a language that belonged on a space ship. The woman responded, and the two pelted each other in rapid-fire Norwegian for a minute.

Mat bent down and whispered to Freddy. The boy nodded, grinning big. Then the family walked off, the boy scurrying to keep up with his parents' long strides.

"What did you say to him?" Luce asked.

"I told him to be careful of the goats on the cable cars."

Mat's eyes twinkled. Luce shook her head and forced herself to look away. Then took a step back. Standing next to him, breathing in his clean, masculine scent was too much. She ran through her checklist once again and busied herself straightening the brochures in the overflowing rack.

"How much longer are you stuck down here?" His voice rippled over her skin and she actually shivered.

"Um, Nora's shift starts in five minutes. She should be here any second. But I don't feel stuck. I kind of like it. The grass is always greener," she chuckled. "When I was down here all I wanted was to make it up there." She tilted her head to the exposed levels of the open courtyard. The offices where they worked were on the fourth floor. "Now I miss the noise, the activity." She shrugged.

"I don't think I could take it." He scanned the crowded tables and lines at the food vendors and shook his head slightly.

"You'd rather be cooped up in front of a computer all day staring at pixels? You might call your job graphic design, but I call it slow torture. Give me the unwashed masses any day. Besides, I would have thought you'd be used to them, with as much traveling as you seem to have done."

"Yeah, I like to observe, not really interact. And the questions you get here..." He trailed off as an irate man stalked to the booth, a sniffling woman in tow.

"She said she wanted to go to Alcatraz." He slapped his hand on the counter. "How could she not know she'd have to take a boat there? It's an island for Chrissakes!"

The pair had the look of newlyweds, with their matching T-shirts and cargo shorts. The young wife dabbed her eyes. "I get seasick," she said softly.

"Well, I already bought the damn tickets! You couldn't have told me about that before?"

"Listen," Luce said, holding the husband's eye. "There's a ticket exchange across the street at the pier." She pulled out a map and highlighted the location. "Go here and you can find someone who wants to go to Alcatraz to take your tickets and you can change them out for something else, maybe a walking tour or a trip to Coit Tower." Luce smiled at the wife.

"I'm afraid of heights," she whispered. Her husband groaned, throwing up his hands in frustration.

"Well, there are lots of other options," Luce said, evenly. "I'm sure you can find something to do that doesn't involve water or heights."

The couple walked away, the man grumbling, the woman cowering. Luce fell into her chair with a sigh, pointedly not looking at Mat. "You may have a point."

Mat snorted, then mimed tipping his hat to her as he ambled off into the lunch crowd. She watched him retreat, allowing herself a few moments to finally gawk at the artistic wonder of his ass filling out his pants.

"You know it's not polite to stare," a voice said from behind her.

Luce jumped, then gave a mock growl as she spun to face her new friend Delilah.

"It's not polite to sneak up on people, and yet you do it to me almost every day."

"It's not my fault that you are extraordinarily jumpy."

"You and your ninja stealth."

"Cat-like reflexes." Delilah grinned and hopped up onto the counter. Her purple dreadlocks flowed down her back in two ponytails and she kicked her legs out, showing off multi-colored striped stockings and silver Doc Martens. "How much longer are you stuck here for?"

"Why does everybody think I'm stuck here?"

Delilah angled her head toward the candy shop she owned. "It's a mad house in there, I need a break. Wanna blow this joint and go to the Crabhouse?"

"You're going to abandon your own store? Sounds unprofessional to me."

She shrugged. "I didn't claim to be a professional, I just make candy. Besides, that's why I hired the minions."

In the mere weeks it had been in operation, Delilah's Candy Bar had become one of the most popular shops in the Button

Factory. Her homemade goodies rivaled the city's more famous candy supplier, Ghirardelli, in taste, plus she had treats no one else could think up: strawberry candy cane spun sugar, blueberry chocolate cups, mango mint licorice. Some of it sounded like it wouldn't work, but once your tongue met her candy, you were convinced she was magic.

"Sorry, I can't bail," Luce said. "Since I was covering down here, I have a ton of work to do upstairs. I'll be eating lunch at my desk today."

Delilah frowned elaborately. Her expressions in general were never limited merely to her face. Usually an elbow or ankle at least was involved. Her makeup always included an intricate design painted on her face in colored sparkles. Luce thought Delilah's ancestry was Chinese, but the woman was always vague about her origins, never speaking of her family or childhood or where she'd lived before arriving in San Francisco a couple of months earlier and opening up a fine establishment specializing in sugared goods.

Once her frown was complete, Delilah hopped off the counter, eyes bright. Her moods shifted rapidly and Luce often had a hard time keeping up.

"Okay, Luce-inda," pronouncing her full name like it was two words, as she tended to. "You go back up to your corporate prison, and I'll have a super fun lunch time without you. Good luck this afternoon. Oh, and watch your head."

With a wink and a twirl she was gone.

Luce followed Delilah's purple hair until it disappeared in the sea of patrons. A five-minute interaction with her friend was exhausting. What did she mean about watching her head? Luce shrugged it off as just another odd Delilah-ism.

She definitely should have paid more attention.

TWO

"CAN I BUG YOU FOR A SECOND?"

Luce paused her contemplation of the ceiling tiles to turn to the doorway.

Mat stood there, phone in hand, an adorably perplexed expression on his face.

"What's up?" she asked, stifling a sigh of exasperation. He had no right to be so charming even when confused.

"Bobby sent a text asking me to go down to the storage room and dig up last year's brochures—apparently there was some kind of misprint?"

"Oh, yeah, they used the old logo, plus the telephone number was wrong. Otherwise they were perfect."

Mat smiled. It was definitely safer to focus her gaze on a spot on his shirt as opposed to being hypnotized by his perfect, even teeth.

"I'm not exactly sure where the storage room is, and Bobby's not great with specifics." He motioned toward his phone.

This time Luce smiled. Their boss was a great guy, but how he ever made it into management was a mystery. He was completely disorganized and mentally scattered—frankly, it was like working for her parents. His text had no doubt been filled with half-formed thoughts and an utter lack of coherency.

"It's in the basement, otherwise known as the crypt."

Mat's eyebrows shot up.

"Didn't you hear—that's where they keep the bodies?"

His lips twisted into a sexy smirk, and she shook her head to dislodge her wayward thoughts. "Don't worry about it, I'll take you down there. The place is kind of twisty and turny. Our storage area is almost impossible to find if you haven't been before."

She led the way to the elevator where they rode down in slightly awkward silence. On the first floor, they wound their way through the light early afternoon crowd to the stairwell leading to the horror movie set the Factory called a basement. The bottom level had not been renovated like the rest of the building and held a snarling labyrinth of corridors and hidden rooms. Needless to say, it wasn't her favorite place.

Most of the center's shops had been assigned storage rooms here, but few used them. The business office, of course, was one of the few. Their room was located at the end of a long and poorly lit hallway. Even with Mat beside her she wished she'd brought her pepper spray.

"Here we go," she said, stopping in front of an enormous metal sliding door. She grabbed the handle and began to pull. The thing had evidently been constructed to withstand a nuclear holocaust; it creaked and groaned its disapproval at being disturbed. Mat reached over her, caging her in his arms as he helped push the door along. When they'd managed it, Luce stepped back into the wall of his chest and stifled a squeak. For the life of her, she couldn't remember her checklist. She definitely wasn't breathing; she should do something about that soon. But maybe asphyxiating would be a kinder way to go. Death by daydreaming about Mat's arms wrapped around her seemed more cruel.

To make matters worse, he placed his hands on her shoulders before removing his chest from her back.

"Thanks," he said, then ducked into the room.

"No problem."

She had a new checklist now with only one thing on it: bring her heartbeat down to an acceptable level. One that would allow some of that blood to flow to the areas of her body that needed it, like her legs, so she could get the hell away from here.

"You good?" she called out.

Mat didn't respond.

"I'll just leave you to it, okay?"

Still nothing.

She stepped into the storeroom, lit only by a few bare lightbulbs in the ceiling. Two tiny, grimy windows near the ceiling obscured more sunlight than they let in. The interior was lined with imposing metal shelves overflowing with boxes of everything under the sun from cleaning supplies and ancient computer equipment to office products and coils of cables. She passed a box inexplicably filled with what looked like old typewriter keys. Ironically, there were no buttons to be found.

She waded past piles of discarded furniture, a few giant canvas bags stenciled with the word "LAUNDRY," and a stack of bicycle tires, when the floor began to move. At first it was a gentle shudder, like a semi-truck passing by, then it grew to a mighty shake.

The shelves surrounding her creaked and groaned, then began depositing their contents on the ground. A large box full of yellowed notepads clunked down on Luce's foot and she screamed.

The emptying shelf wobbled on sturdy legs and tipped toward her. Her foot was trapped, pinned under the box, and she watched in slow motion as the shelf, which definitely weighed more than she did, tilted toward her head.

Mat appeared out of nowhere and dove for her. The force of his tackle freed her foot and they fell just out of reach of the toppling shelf of death. She didn't have to remind herself to breathe this time—her lungs were gasping in as much oxygen as they could. In fact, she was in danger of hyperventilating.

Before she could even process how much of his body was in contact with hers, he rose to his knees. He wrapped an arm around her, half-crawling, half-dragging her toward the center of the room, away from the falling shelves and underneath a rusted metal desk. Luce squeezed her eyes shut and curled her body into a ball in the small space. Her foot throbbed. She shivered uncontrollably.

The rumbling stopped several hours later. Or rather several seconds later, but they were the longest of her life.

"Was that your first earthquake?" she asked once her breathing had slowed enough to allow speech.

Though her eyes were still closed, she felt a movement beside her that could have been Mat shaking his head. "I lived in the North Bay for a while growing up, and went through a few in Asia. But you never really get used to them."

She nodded, or at least thought she was nodding, but for some reason her entire body was still convulsing. Goosebumps covered her bare arms. She squeezed them around her knees and tightened every muscle to stop the shaking but couldn't manage it.

Mat's arm slid around her. She leaned into him, grateful for the warmth, though it wasn't the cold that was bothering her. They sat in silence, him rubbing her arms gently until, finally, her trembling subsided.

"Thanks." She pulled away and scooted out from under the desk. Her foot was beginning to swell already. She rotated her ankle gingerly and wiggled her blue-painted toes, extraordinarily glad that she'd splurged for a pedicure the week before.

Mat slid out beside her, staring at her foot. "May I?" he asked. Before she could answer, or mentally run down the pros and cons of allowing any further skin to skin contact, his hands were on her foot, squeezing gently and tilting it back and forth.

Her ankle definitely hurt, but his hands sliding across the sensitive soles of her feet was way more stimulating than painful. Screw the checklist, she couldn't stop herself from staring at his fingers touching her. When he skimmed her arch, she hissed in a breath, then let out a giggle. His brows rose in question.

"That tickled."

His eyes grew dark and mischievous; she could almost see him tucking that bit of information away for the future.

"I don't think it's broken," he said, pulling his hands away. A wave of relief surged through her, mixed with only the tiniest bit of disappointment.

"But maybe I should bow out of that marathon I've been training for?"

He smiled, then sat back on his haunches regarding the area. It had been a disaster zone before the earthquake; now it was post-apocalyptic. The contents of virtually every shelf had been vomited onto the ground. They sat in front of the old desk on the only spot with a clearly visible floor, an island in a sea of detritus.

The force of the quake had also slid the main door shut, but more than that, two of the heavy shelves had fallen in front of it, blocking their exit. There was no way to move the shelves. Luce wondered how they'd all gotten down here in the first place or whether the building had been built around them.

Climbing over them was a possibility, but when Mat tried, he couldn't reach the handle. Luce suspected even if he could, he wouldn't have enough leverage to wrench open the door.

He sat down next to her, covered in sweat and dust and more gorgeous than ever because of it. He pulled his cell phone from his pocket, but there were no bars, either due to their subterranean status or as a result of the lines being overloaded from the earthquake fallout. Luce's phone was upstairs at her desk.

"Looks like we're stuck," he said, putting the phone away.

Great.

THREE

STUCK.

In the creepy storage room.

With Mat.

There was no upside to this situation. Yes, she had delicious man-candy to stare at, but she wasn't supposed to be staring. The checklist forbade it. Not falling into a puddle at the man's feet was a top priority.

There was no way she was going out like Farrah, the HR manager. Farrah was pushing forty, and while she had a certain MILFy quality to her that left her with no shortage of dates, there was an edge of desperation setting in. On Mat's first day, Farrah had wasted no time in letting the entire office know that she was in hot pursuit. It was just embarrassing.

Mat was nice about withstanding the assault. He'd never taken Farrah up on her offers, but he didn't seem to mind her rubbing her boobs all over him under the guise of a friendly hug.

So what if he was sexy, strong, talented, and spoke a weird foreign language? Luce had never been into the sort of guys everyone else liked. Where's the fun in that? She favored the road less traveled. Give her an underdog any day—those were the guys who could really appreciate her. The beautiful people were too high maintenance. She wanted to make sure her dreams were possible no matter what Don Quixote might say. Mathias Woodson was definitely a windmill and she was determined to tilt her black ass in the opposite direction.

Now that the ground seemed stable, she and Mat sat with their backs against the desk they'd taken cover under. Luce's foot was propped on top of a stack of telephone books he'd dug out. She searched for a way to break the silence. Who knew how long they'd be stuck down here? Best to make nice.

"So," she racked her brain for an innocuous topic. "It seems like you've traveled a lot."

"Yeah, pretty much non-stop since I graduated high school. I like new places—staying still has always felt so confining, you know?"

Luce nodded, though she didn't really know. Staying in one place had always been a comfort for her, as opposed to being dragged all over the country by her parents. Still, she was aiming for agreeable, stuck-in-the-basement conversation, not a rehash of her crazy childhood.

"Where have you been?"

"I try to change countries every four to five months. I just got back from Brazil, before that was Turkey, Italy, Morocco, and South Africa."

"Wow, how do you do that? Where do you stay?"

He shrugged. "Hostels usually at first. After that, most places have some version of a Craigslist where you can find people looking for roommates or sublets. There's kind of a network of ex-pats who have their ear to the ground. I always find something."

"And you just freelance?"

"Yeah, sometimes finding an internet connection is the hardest part, but in the past few years it's been less of an issue. I stick to the major cities when I'm working on a project and do more exploring in my free time."

Luce's passport was blank. She wasn't averse to the idea of vacation travel—it actually sounded great. Her childhood excursions had been limited by her father's fear of planes and trains. The plane thing she could almost understand, but who was afraid of trains? She'd thought this promotion—more money, dedicated vacation days—would afford her the chance to finally see the world. But then her dad had gotten sick.

"So you don't have a home base anywhere?"

"My sister, Charlotte, still lives here, up in Hill Valley. So I usually come to visit her at least once a year. But I don't have an apartment or anything. Usually I just crash on her couch."

"How old are you?"

He turned to meet her eyes, his expression guarded. "Twenty-eight."

She'd thought he was younger, he had such a youthful face and his lifestyle seemed like that of someone just out of college, determined to see the world before settling down.

"Do you think you'll ever stop and have, you know, a regular life?"

"What do you mean regular?" Now he sounded a bit ticked off.

"You know, *normal*. A normal life with a car and a job and a mortgage. Kids, picket fences, the whole thing." She swirled her hand around.

"Normal would be death. I can't imagine how people do it— go to the same job every day for decades? It's so soul stealing. Life-stealing. I think normal is for suckers."

Luce kept her expression neutral. In a second, Mat seemed to hear what he'd said and a contrite expression came across his face.

"I didn't mean—"

"No, it's okay. I get it." She was nodding like a bobble-head, but couldn't stop herself. "You sound just like my parents. They were always trying to fight the system, go against the grain, and do things their own way. We lived in a van for two years. They wanted to live in a treehouse, but Child Protective Services didn't think kindly of that idea."

She didn't mention that *she* had been the one to call CPS on her own parents at the age of eleven. Somehow she didn't think Mat would sympathize. He likely would have appreciated her unconventional upbringing.

"Normal might be for suckers, but when you're a kid who's got to take care of herself from practically the time she's born, then you may wish for a little normal."

After that she couldn't think of anything else to say. So much for agreeable conversation. Luce didn't feel bad for challenging Mat's assumptions—people like him never thought any further than their own excitement or idea of happiness. Others rarely came into the equation. What Luce hated more than anything else was selfishness. She'd been surrounded by it her entire life.

Even now, as she paid most of her parents' expenses, made sure her dad took his medication and didn't miss his doctor appointments, she wondered what it would be like to not have to take care of everything. To have someone care more about her than about themselves.

She sighed, repositioning herself on the uncomfortable concrete floor. Maybe one day she'd find out. She looked over at Mat. He was so beautiful—perfect lips, perfect smile, perfect ass. Genuinely nice. Good with kids. A really decent guy. But under all of that was someone whose big picture was a little too self-centered.

She didn't think she'd need her checklist any more. Now that she knew what was beneath the surface, looking-but-not-touching would be easy.

Forty-seven hours later—or maybe ninety minutes—a jangle at the door alerted them to their rescue.

"Hello?" a muffled voice called out.

Luce stood, balancing on her good leg. Mat popped up and shouted. The massive sliding door wrenched open; behind it were Randy, another security guard, and a beaming Delilah.

Mat helped Luce climb over the toppled shelves and out into the hallway, which appeared far less scary now that it held salvation. Luce collapsed into Delilah's open arms wanting to cry.

"There, there," Delilah said, patting her head granny style.

"Thank God!" Luce exclaimed. "I thought they were going to find our dry bones centuries from now in some sort of archeological dig."

"Dramatic much?" Delilah said. "I peeped you going down here before the seismic plates hit the fan. It just took a while to clear everything out upstairs and calm folks down. Hasn't anybody ever been through an earthquake before?" She rolled her eyes. "So," she said, drawing out the word and waggling her eyebrows suggestively in Mat's direction. He stood several feet away talking to Randy.

"Ugh, no. Not even."

Delilah executed a miniature frown. "Wait, what happened? Sweetie, if you couldn't make it work trapped in a storage room all damsel in distress-like, I don't know what to do with you."

Luce led her farther down the hall. "He and I are not compatible. Big picture, world-view type stuff. Republican-Democrat type stuff."

Delilah gasped. "He's a Republican?"

"No, I mean I don't know, doubtful, but he might as well be. He's just an overgrown child with no responsibilities and no desire for any, and I already have two sixty-year-old children. I don't need another adult to take care of."

Luce threaded her arm through Delilah's and limped toward the stairwell, eager to be out of the dungeon.

FOUR

"PLAY IT AGAIN," Charlotte said, her smile set to one thousand watts.

Mat sighed and restarted the video from the beginning. He sat next to his sister in her tiny kitchen, hunched over her laptop, watching the video for the fifth time.

"It already has over ten thousand views and it's only been up two days!" Charlotte rocked back and forth with excitement.

"How many of those views are you?" Mat teased, wrapping an arm around her. He'd never seen his sister look so happy, which was saying a lot. Charlotte's natural facial expression was a smile, but for the last two days she'd been glowing with joy. Her curly hair teetered haphazardly in a messy bun on the top of her head, and her eyes shone with delight as she showed off the impressive ring weighing down her finger.

"Micah had been planning it for weeks," she said, sparkling just as brightly as her diamond. "Almost since we first met."

On the video, Micah, Charlotte's musician boyfriend of one year, sat on a bicycle with a guitar, strumming while pedaling with no hands. He sang a very silly song about Charlotte and how much he loved her, rhyming her name with "harlot," "varmint," and "marmoset."

As he wound his way through Golden Gate park, costumed dancers popped out from behind trees singing verses and performing choreographed steps. At the song's finale, several dozen people crowded the screen singing and dancing in unison. Micah stopped the bike and remained balanced as he sang the last verse, rhyming "verily" with "marry me." The camera panned around to reveal a very teary Charlotte sitting on a golf cart, watching the show first-hand. Micah got on one knee and placed the two-carat diamond on her slender finger.

"Seriously, though. I'm impressed. Micah's a great guy. With a lot of crazy friends." Mat reached for his mug of coffee next to the computer.

Charlotte admired her ring, her eyes a little wistful. "Yeah, he's amazing. Of course I haven't said yes yet."

Mat choked, nearly spitting the coffee onto the computer. "What? Why not? I thought you were madly in love."

"I am, of course I am. I can't imagine being with anyone else."

"So what is it?"

"You know he'll be on tour half of the year. Europe then Asia."

Micah was the drummer for the band RiotSphere, who'd had a track go viral the year before. When Charlotte met him, he'd been back home in Hill Valley, considering leaving the group. But after the lead singer left to go solo, Micah's other bandmates had begged him to return. They'd been in the studio for the past few months recording their next album with Charlotte helping to pen some of the tracks.

"I just don't think a long-distance relationship can work. I mean, look what happened with Mom and Dad, right?"

"Well, why don't you go with him?" Mat asked. "I don't get it. Is it your job?"

"No, my boss is fine with me being a virtual assistant. And I can work on my screenplay from anywhere, I just...." She twisted the ring on her finger once, then turned her gaze to him. She looked so much like their mother with her blonde hair and green eyes, it still sometimes startled him. Her skin was golden brown, so light it could pass for a perpetual tan, and many people didn't realize she was half-black.

Mat was a few shades darker, but knew well the stigma of being thought as "not black enough." He'd gotten the sense that the feeling of not being accepted, or being sought after for the wrong reasons, had seeped into Charlotte's relationships. Her ex had cheated on her with one of her close friends, so Mat was glad she'd found Micah. He was a really good guy and great for Charlotte. So her reluctance to accept his proposal just didn't make sense.

"Just tell me, Char," he prompted.

"I don't know if I can just abandon you." She suddenly looked so much younger than thirty-four, but the heaviness in her eyes was old.

"What do you mean, abandon me? I'm hardly ever in one place for long anyway. I can always visit you wherever you are."

Charlotte stopped fidgeting with her ring, and her expression turned serious. He knew that look all too well—she wanted to talk about "his future."

"I'm worried about you," she said as he groaned internally. "One day, hopefully soon, you're going to want to stop being a nomad and settle down somewhere. There can't be too many places you haven't been yet, right?"

Mat snorted. "The world is a big place, Char."

"I know, I know, and traveling has its merits, but it's important to have a home base somewhere—to be settled. I just don't know how I can run off on tour with a rock band and leave you with nowhere to come home to."

Mat stilled, regarding his sister through fresh eyes. "Is that why you've stayed here in the Bay Area so long? To give me a place to come back to?" Charlotte's averted eyes gave him his answer.

"Char, I never wanted you to put anything on hold for me—especially not getting married. I'm a grown-up and I love you and appreciate your concern, but I'm not your responsibility anymore."

"You're my brother and I love you and want you to be happy. I've been taking care of you forever. I don't really know how to stop." Her sad smile broke his heart, especially since he was the reason for erasing the joy from a few minutes before. "I can't help worrying. You don't have any close friends, no girlfriend, just temporary, freelance design gigs for income. It's always been the two of us, we've always depended on each other. With Dad being—" she waved her hand in the air, "— the way he is, and Mom and her shiny new family, how could I live with myself if I left you too? Everybody needs somewhere to come home to."

She shook her head when Mat tried to speak. "I know you think I'm a crazy worry-wart. I don't need a lecture on the convenience of modern travel." Her eyes teared up. "And I know you're not the same little kid who fell apart when Mom left. But ever since that day I've made sure you had a home. You might not think you need it, but I know you do. I know how you look when you get off a plane from God knows where, and I see the change that happens while you're here. A part of that little boy is still inside of you, and I promised him I'd never abandon him. No matter what."

Her face was wet as she pulled him into an embrace. "It would be different if you had someone," she whispered into his neck.

Mat couldn't stand seeing Charlotte cry. He hated the guilt that gnawed at him, threatening to tear him open from the inside out. He did owe her. When their mom left, their dad had been deployed. What started as a weekend trip back home to Norway kept being extended longer and longer. She would call and promise she was coming back in a few days, and then never show up.

They had been convinced their father didn't know. He never mentioned anything in their infrequent phone calls, and since she claimed to be coming back, they never said anything. After a few weeks, her phone calls stopped. Calls to their grandparents' house in Oslo went unanswered. Messages unreturned.

Ten-year-old Mat began failing classes, getting into fights, stealing. He grew more withdrawn until he was just a ball of anger looking for an outlet. When their dad finally returned home, Mat had assumed they would pick up the broken pieces of their family and put them back together in a new formation. A puzzle, slightly skewed, some of the parts in the wrong place, but still something.

But their dad poured himself into his job. They moved again, and then again, as he sought higher rank. Within a year, Mat was lucky if he saw his father once a week. It was Charlotte who'd calm his sudden rages. She studied child psychology books and pelted him with art supplies until he finally began to draw and found a way to manage his emotions.

She signed the permission slips, made dinner, helped with his homework. Came to his art shows and basketball games. She'd postponed college until he graduated from high school and was probably the only reason he'd finished school at all.

And he'd thanked her by taking off the first chance he could, never realizing she was still putting her life on hold so he'd always have a place to retreat to.

Overgrown child. Another adult to take care of. He'd overheard Luce talking with Delilah after their rescue the other day. The words stung. He hadn't meant to antagonize her. Even now, the soft fruit and cocoa butter scent surrounding her licked at his senses.

He'd noticed her velvety, dark chocolate skin and full, sensual lips the first day he started work, though unlike some of the other women there, she was not in obvious pursuit of him. That was for the best—he'd learned not to shit where he ate. Workplace romances got complicated, and he avoided complicated at all costs.

Anything more than a brief fling was off-limits. He'd tried the girlfriend thing. Dated a graduate student in Italy for close to three months. When it was time for him to go, he'd even asked her to come with him. But she had roots, a family, a thesis to finish. Sure, he could have stayed, but then what? Eventually, something would happen to tear them apart. *Der gror ikke mose på rullande stein.* A rolling stone gathers no moss. He learned that from his mother.

The only one he'd ever counted on was Charlotte.

She loved him unconditionally, and would continue to put her life on hold while he figured out his. If he let that happen, he deserved to be chewed apart by the gnawing jaws of guilt. He would deserve so much worse.

When she was with Micah, it was like she was the person she was always meant to be. He had to figure out how to convince her that he would be all right.

It would be different if you had someone.

Mat squeezed his sister. "Listen." His mind raced, traveling a little slower than his mouth. "I wasn't gonna tell you until I was —until we—but, well, there's this girl…"

Charlotte let out a squeak and pulled back, wiping her nose and eyes. "Who is she? Why am I just hearing about this? When do I get to meet her?"

"Well—we've only been out a few times, so I didn't want to jinx it by telling you about her, but she's pretty amazing. I think it might be serious."

"Where did you meet her? At work?" Charlotte asked, her smile erasing all traces of tears.

"Yeah." Mat nodded, pushing aside the murmurings of his conscience.

"What's her name?" Charlotte asked.

Her name.

Mat replied with the only name he could think of, regretting it as soon as the word passed his lips. "Luce, her name is Luce."

Charlotte was glowing again. "Luce. I like her already."

FIVE

LUCE WALKED BACK to her office from the copy room, arms laden with the collated and stapled budget packets she'd spent the last forty-five minutes putting together. Weren't there interns who did this kind of thing? She stopped just in front of her door as an unfamiliar woman approached.

"Can I help you?" she asked.

The woman smiled, and Luce instantly liked her. She was gorgeous, but with her simple, slouchy clothes and messy bun, you could tell she didn't pay much attention to her appearance.

"I'm looking for Lucinda Garvey."

"That's me."

"Luce!" The woman's smile grew impossibly larger, like she'd just met her oldest friend after years apart.

"Um, hi." Luce motioned to her office and set her papers down on her desk. As soon as her arms were clear, the woman pulled her into a huge bear hug. Her tiny arms were surprisingly strong.

On the other hand, maybe the woman's appearance was less "I don't care" and more "I'm crazy."

Luce pulled back. "Um—have we met?"

The woman laughed. "Sorry, I'm Charlotte. I was just so excited I couldn't wait to meet you. I know I shouldn't bug you at work."

Luce kept smiling, racking her brain for knowledge of anyone called Charlotte. This woman couldn't be crazy—no mentally ill people sported ice like the one weighing down Charlotte's ring finger, right? She decided to play along, hoping she hadn't forgotten anyone important.

"Sit down, please."

"So you're coming this weekend?" Charlotte asked.

Luce took a deep breath and realized she wasn't going to be able to play along after all. "I'm sorry, what's happening this weekend?"

Charlotte's face morphed to shock. "Mat didn't tell you?"

Mat. Didn't he mention a sister called Charlotte? There was some resemblance now that she looked harder.

"I haven't seen Mat yet today."

"Oh," Charlotte's smile returned. "Let me send you the invite. Once I finally said yes to Micah, he found out the record company had scheduled a couple of tour dates in the U.S. The first one's in Vegas, so we're actually getting married in two weeks!" She jumped up and down. "Anyway, the ceremony is going to be really tiny, so Micah's mother is insisting we have this blowout engagement party with our family and friends *this* weekend in Napa. She rented out an entire vineyard for it and everything." She took a deep breath. "So what's your email?"

Luce was going to have to put crazy back on the table as a possibility, but Charlotte was so nice, so friendly, so amazingly excited, that Luce didn't want to burst the bubble she was living in. And it's not like her email address was a social security number. How much damage could the woman do?

Still, something weird was going on and she wanted to get to the bottom of it. After Charlotte finished typing, Luce said, "You know, why don't we go see Mat right now? You can't stop by without visiting him, right?"

"Of course not. He's not too busy, do you think?"

"Too busy for his sister?"

They rose and made their way down the hall to the cubicle where Mat sat, his back to them, headphones on. Charlotte snuck up behind him and covered his eyes with her hands. He spun around, pulling off his headphones, then froze when he saw Luce standing behind his sister.

"Hey," he said looking back and forth between the two women.

"Look who I found in the hallway," Luce said in a sing-song voice, crossing her arms. "And why am I just hearing about this whole Napa thing now?" She put a note of playful censure into her voice, but her eyes bored holes into Mat.

He stood, hugged his sister then moved to stand awkwardly beside Luce.

"Can I get a picture of you guys?" Charlotte asked, giddy. "I've never had one of Mat and his girlfriend."

Mat turned to stone beside her, and Luce kept her face neutral, only by virtue of the fact that she had so many years of practice dealing with unexplained occurrences caused by her parents.

"By all means, take a picture of Mat with his girlfriend. Can I be in it too?"

"Oh, I like her," Charlotte said, laughing, and raised her phone. "Closer you guys."

Mat slid closer and put an arm around Luce. His smile was tight as the shutter sound clicked.

"I'm going to let you guys get back to work. It was so wonderful meeting you, Luce!"

Charlotte pulled Luce in for another massive hug.

"You too." Despite the fact that she was going to murder her brother in short order, Luce really did like Charlotte.

"I'll see you next weekend."

Luce smiled and nodded, but didn't respond. With a hug and a kiss for Mat, Charlotte was gone in a whirlwind of strawberry shampoo.

Luce turned on Mat just as the receptionist, Mina, sauntered down the hallway, swaying her hips seductively and pulling down the hem of her V neck sweater to expose more of her cleavage. Luce rolled her eyes.

"Hi, Mat," she said, actually batting her eyelashes.

Mat nodded tightly, barely looking at her.

"Um, I was wondering if you could help me with something. It's a Photoshop thing, and I know you're the expert."

Mina was shameless. It's like she had her own clichéd flirting checklist. Toss hair, check. Bite lip, check. Luce waited for her to run her hand over her breasts to complete the ridiculousness.

"Hi, Mina," Luce said. The younger woman finally noticed Luce and waved in her direction.

"So, Mat, whenever, you know, you get a chance," Mina said.

"Sure, I'll come by later."

"Thanks, so much!" She sauntered closer and ran her hand down his biceps. Then she spun, her flared skirt twirling up almost revealing her underwear—if she was wearing any. If she sashayed any harder walking away she would probably sprain something.

"Oh, Luce," she called over her shoulder. "Bobby wanted me to tell you the budget meeting's in five minutes."

Luce rolled her eyes, then turned back to Mat. She pointed her finger at him, but the words wouldn't come. "I don't even have time for this right now."

He started to speak but she cut him off. "After work. The Candy Bar."

He closed his mouth and nodded. She shook her head and went back to her office.

As she stacked the budget reports and put them in manila

folders, one thought circled her mind over and over. Why did Mat involve *her* in his little scheme—whatever it was?

Delilah's Candy Bar was set up like an actual bar, with bartenders serving candy cocktails and assorted treats. There was a self-service section on the opposite wall where customers could fill bags full of sweets and pay by the pound.

Luce sat at the bar, sipping a delicious white chocolate virgin martini. The concoction was normally a guaranteed pick me up, but it wasn't doing the trick this evening.

She felt Mat's arrival, could tell he was looking at her based on how she suddenly felt flushed, her skin too hot and tight. She swiveled on the bar stool to monitor his approach—slow, as if he was nearing a wild animal. He sat next to her.

Luce waited for him to say something. She refused to be the one to break the silence.

"I'm really sorry," he said, finally. "This whole thing got kinda out of hand."

"You think?"

Some of her icy anger melted at the sincerity in his expression. Like a faucet opening, he poured out the story of Charlotte's impending marriage and how she would only say yes if she felt that he was settled. His mouth had gotten him into trouble, and he'd said Luce's name in a fit of desperation. He hadn't been prepared for how very much Charlotte would want to meet her.

"My sister, she practically raised me. She's given up a lot for me and I just…I wanted to reassure her. I'm really sorry."

Luce gripped onto her empty martini glass. "I just don't understand…. Why me?"

He turned to her, a curious expression on his face.

"I mean, I'm sure Mina would do a great job being your pretend girlfriend. Or Farrah. I'm sure either one of them would be—very thorough." Luce pushed away the image that threatened to surface.

Mat frowned. "I don't really know why. Your name was just the first to come into my head."

Luce sat back in her seat. There was no wacky romantic comedy setup; he didn't secretly have feelings for her. He literally just said the first name that popped into his head. What did she expect?

"Charlotte really likes you."

She turned to him, incredulous. "She's pretty awesome, but there's no way I can pretend to be your girlfriend for an entire weekend. You get that, right?"

"Yeah, sure. Of course." He sat back. "It's just she really likes you. She texted me that she thinks you're a good influence on me."

"So I'll be your mentor. Train you in the ways of responsible human behavior. Teach you to use the Force. But your girlfriend? Mat, seriously."

"Do you want money?"

She guffawed. "You're trying to buy me? Why don't you go find a call girl? Tell Charlotte that we broke up but you've found a new love of your life." She stood in a huff.

"Luce, wait, I didn't mean it like that." He reached out and held her elbow—his touch was like an anchor weighing her feet to the ground. "Is there anything that would make you agree to this? I know it's asking a lot."

She wrenched free of his grip, her skin tingling from the lost contact. She couldn't look at him. She wanted to help, and couldn't bear the thought of someone as sweet as Charlotte missing out on the love of her life, as improbable as it was—but this really wasn't going to work.

"I'm really sorry, Mat. I want to be able to help, I just can't. I think you need to tell your sister the truth."

He nodded slowly, rising. "No, I understand. I shouldn't

have gotten you involved. *I'm* sorry." With a final look he turned and left the store.

"How do I get into these situations?" Luce said, dropping her head into her hands. "Is this officially a fiasco?"

The jingling of bells announced Delilah's arrival across the bar. "I think it would need to be way wackier to reach fiasco territory. It sounds like he was in a bind."

Luce looked up. "A bind? And now I'm expected to take part in some kind of romantic comedy premise? It's insane. I think the sanity of that entire family should be called into question." Luce shook her head. "Do you really think she'll call off the wedding if she finds out Mat doesn't have a girlfriend?"

"You did say she was crazy."

Luce drained her sugartini and shook her head. "It doesn't make any sense."

"Would you take off on a world tour and leave your parents to fend for themselves? If your dad wasn't sick, but they were still..."

"Emotional infants? Unable to manage even the remote semblance of a normal adult thought process?" Luce's shoulders sagged. "But Mat is functional."

"Your parents have managed to keep themselves alive for sixty years."

"Barely," Luce muttered.

"Besides, didn't you always want a life full of adventure?"

Luce stared at her. "No. I wanted a life full of normalcy. Regular school. Bedtimes. Running water. I've had quite enough adventure."

Delilah stared meaningfully at Luce. "PR normal? Budget report normal? Don't you miss the drama just a teeny, tiny bit?"

Luce was unwilling to admit any truth to Delilah's assertions. Yes, her job was just the teensiest bit boring, and yes she missed the hustle and bustle of being in the thick of things at the info desk downstairs. She'd even thought it might be nice to work for one of the tour companies, leading visitors around the city she'd claimed as her own after her parents had finally settled in one place.

Luce shook her head. "It's too much. Besides, all that deception just doesn't sit right with me." She tapped her fingers on the bar before rising to leave. The last thing she needed was another fiasco.

SIX

LUCE DROPPED her keys on the entry table in her parents' hallway and slumped against the wall. The smell of smoke filled the apartment.

"Joyce!" The apartment was cluttered, as usual. It was saved from official hoarder status because of Luce's careful ministrations. She waded through, picking up trash, pushing shoes and cartons out of the way until she reached the bedroom in the back.

Her father, Moses, sat in his wheelchair next to the open window, hastily stubbing out a cigarette. Joyce sat next to him, looking guilty.

Luce sighed. "Didn't the doctor tell you just this last week? No. More. Cigarettes."

She grabbed the package on the window sill, a new one since she'd just done a sweep the day before, and stuffed it in her pocket.

"And you!" she turned to her mother. Joyce looked away sheepishly.

"I've already got the damn 'zema," Moses said. "So why can't I keep smoking?"

Luce stalked over and picked up her father's oxygen mask, handing it to him. He grumbled as he stuck the tubes into his nose. "This doggone thing is uncomfortable as hell."

"Good," she said, picking up the ashtray and dumping it into the trash.

"Mom, you can't keep buying him cigarettes. This has to stop. Did you listen to anything the doctor said?"

"The doctor said he was getting worse," her mother chirped. "There's no cure for COPD, so he may as well smoke while he's still here."

"Do you even want to still be here?" She rounded on her father.

He sat there wheezing, his eyes watering. A round of coughing was about to start. She moved the box of tissues closer to him so he could catch the blood and mucus his lungs were spewing out. She didn't want to watch though.

As she left the room, her mother spoke loudly over her father's coughing fit. "I'll never understand why that gal takes things so seriously. She could suck the fun out of anything."

Luce headed to the kitchen to make sure there was food in the fridge. She found a few cartons of takeout that smelled relatively edible.

"I'm leaving!" she called, sticking her head back through the bedroom doorway.

"Good riddance!" her father said, turning away to stare out the window. Her mother shrugged her shoulders as if to say, *You know how your father is.* Absolving herself of any responsibility. As usual.

Luce locked their door and trudged up the stairs to her apartment. But before she'd made it a few steps, her mother's voice rose behind her.

"I forgot to tell you. The landlord called and said that he was finally going to fumigate our apartment this weekend. Dad and I will need to stay with you for a couple of days."

Luce's knuckles cracked. She looked down to find that her

fists were clenched so tightly she was in danger of losing feeling in her fingers.

"Why does your apartment need to be fumigated?" Her jaw ached from the tension of forcing the words through closed teeth.

Her mother twisted one of the rings that decorated each of her fingers. "I may have found a pizza box that I'd forgotten about."

"Found it where?"

"Possibly under the bed." Her mother's eyes darted around. "And covered in roaches."

Luce felt a gush of air escape from her body.

"It'sjustacoupleofdays. It'llbelikeoldtimes." Joyce's words rushed together in one big jumble and then she was gone. Slamming the door before Luce could even respond.

Luce shut her eyes and counted to ten. She'd lived here since her last year of college, the top floor of an adorable duplex. Once her father's COPD had gotten severe and her parents had been kicked out of yet another apartment, Luce had talked to her landlord and arranged to have her parents move in downstairs when the old tenant left.

Taking care of them was almost a full-time job, and most days, she didn't know why she bothered. They were never grateful, they never saw her as a loving daughter, just a nagging inconvenience out to spoil their carefree lifestyle. Though how carefree they could be in the face of her father's debilitating illness was unknown.

She paid their rent, made sure they had enough food, took her dad to the doctor, and made sure he took his medicine. She tried to keep him from smoking and doing the other things that would exacerbate his condition. And for all that, she got nothing in return. Not even an *I love you.*

Once inside her own apartment, she sank onto her couch and toed off her shoes. Her ankle was still sore, but the swelling had gone down and she could walk without a problem. She rubbed the joint until the acheyness abated. The last thing she needed was an injury.

A boyfriend, on the other hand, would be nice. A real one, not the acting challenge that Mat offered. Someone to rub her hurt ankle. Ask about her day. She sighed, leaning back.

She'd always sought out the most normal, stable men she could find. Accountants. Law students. Insurance guys. The only problem with these guys was they didn't have much to talk about outside of work, sports, and television. Luce knew that if she kept at it she could find someone both interesting and reliable. When she did, she wouldn't let him go.

As a lonely kid, she'd been shuffled around while her father tried his best to make a living without actually having a job. Before she was born, he'd been a poet and taught college-level poetry, which was where he'd met her mother, who'd been going back to school after years away. Even though the age difference wasn't significant, the university frowned on professor-student relationships and he was fired. After that, the two of them decided that the system was for suckers.

They traveled the country. Sometimes he'd pick up an adjunct professor gig for a semester or two, but inevitably there was some reason why that particular institution was not right for him.

He'd made a name for himself in the seventies with his black-power poetry, and had been paid to speak and lecture. He also wrote manifestos and editorial think pieces on a range of social topics.

Her mother had dropped out of college the first time to model. After meeting Moses and dropping out again, she just followed wherever he went. Her official job, Luce always thought, was hype-woman. You know how rappers always have someone else on stage with them hyping up the crowd, getting them to throw their hands in the air and shout and all that? That was Joyce's specialty. She served as barker for his public lectures, enticing folks to come up and hear him speak. At poetry readings, she was always engaging the crowd. She was good with people—that's where Luce got it from—but her work ethic beyond her husband's career was nil.

The thought of the two of them infecting the peace Luce had painstakingly created in her home with all of their noise and smoke and messiness—*roaches? Seriously?* — was not something she was ready to even consider.

If the two of them were going to invade her apartment for an entire weekend, then Luce needed to be far, far away.

Like Napa? She shushed the little voice inside her head. It was evil and traitorous and...and...just plain mean. Besides, Napa wasn't even that far away. And Luce wasn't a wine drinker. She hated the heady, briny smell of the stuff. She barely liked grapes when they weren't fermented—what would she do in Napa for an entire weekend?

Have a free vacation. Relax. Be away from Moses and Joyce. Would those two be able to survive for two days without her? She sniffed.

Maybe she could convince Delilah to come and look in on them at least once.

Besides, there were other things to do in Napa besides drink wine. And Charlotte was so sweet. Letting her live under the delusion that her brother was getting himself together and turning into a responsible person in a real relationship wasn't the worst thing in the world. Anything for love, right?

The idea of spending a weekend with Mat was daunting, but Luce had faced tougher obstacles in life. She'd worked her way through college and was well on her way to being the master of her own destiny.

She grabbed her phone and pulled up the company phone list.

So what if her greatest acting accomplishment thus far was playing a tree in her sixth-grade play? She'd made one awesome tree. Pretending to be Mat's girlfriend couldn't be that much harder, could it?

SEVEN

ON FRIDAY AFTERNOON, sitting in the passenger seat of a rented sedan, Luce was entranced by the beauty of the vineyards spreading out around them. She could feel the stress melt away from her body with each passing mile. Her last vacation had been exactly never, so she was determined to cherish this short weekend away from responsibility. But a little tendril of guilt wiggled in, threading its way through the peace that had started to build.

She and Mat would be lying to his sister Charlotte and her friends, pretending to be boyfriend and girlfriend. She told herself it was a harmless white lie with no malice intended. Charlotte was just overly concerned about her brother's well-being. Seeing him settled down with a girlfriend would ease her mind enough to let her go on tour with her rock star fiancé guilt-free. Luce was actually doing a good deed. But her conscience was not quite on board.

She hated lying. And she wasn't entirely sure she could pull this off. If her own parents' irresponsible life choices hadn't pushed her to the point of nearly developing an ulcer, she never would have agreed to this ridiculous ruse.

She chanced a glance over at Mat. His brow descended as he checked the map on his phone. They were close to the inn where the weekend-long engagement party was being held. And though it went against the rules she'd set when she first met him, she couldn't stop staring at his profile.

There was no doubt he was yummy. Far too yummy to ever be her *actual* boyfriend. His naturally golden skin was sun-toasted, and the dusting of stubble on his jaw called to her fingers. She curled them into a tight ball. Forced her gaze away from his face only to get snagged by his hands, loosely gripping the steering wheel.

A flashback struck her: those fingers stroking her bare foot, assessing it for injury after the earthquake they'd been caught in. That was the first time, and last, he'd ever touched her, but she couldn't push the sensation from her mind. If she concentrated, she could still feel his skin on hers.

Goosebumps rose along her exposed flesh. She closed her eyes to relive that moment and when she opened them again, the car was stopped.

"Did I fall asleep?" she asked, stretching her neck and looking around. "Are we here?"

"This is it. The Entwined Vine Inn." They both leaned forward to stare out the windshield. The party was being held in a quaint three-story Victorian set right in the middle of a vine-yard. On one side of the house was a brick patio, its portico strung with paper lanterns. On the other side, the field of greenery stretched out to the horizon. Everything about this place screamed relaxing.

"Micah's mother is paying to rent out the whole thing?" Luce's voice was awed.

"Yeah, though Charlotte said he was going to insist on paying her back. One of the band's unreleased songs got picked up for a commercial. Plus, they'll be touring for the next year and will probably make more money than God."

He grinned and her belly swooped. Nope, couldn't happen.

They had to pretend to be together in front of everyone else, but if she kept on pretending when they were alone, it could only end badly. For her. She summoned a glare, resulting in a confused expression from Mat.

"What?"

She fished her sunglasses out of her bag and attacked her face with them. "Nothing. Let's get on with this." Then she got out of the car and steeled her spine.

Breathe, blink, don't stare and don't get lost in his smile. She could do this.

She hoped.

The inn's lobby was bustling with people. Charlotte was nowhere in sight, but several tattooed and pierced rock star types lounged around. Mat was introducing her to Micah's bandmates when the innkeeper, an efficient-looking woman in her fifties, approached.

"Welcome, welcome. You must be Charlotte's brother and his plus one. Let me show you to your room."

The wide hallway was decorated in florals and dark wood. The innkeeper led them to the last door, a corner room with eggshell blue walls and matching gold damask comforter and curtains. Both the bedroom and the attached bath were tiny. There was just enough space for the queen-sized bed, night-stands, and vanity, but nothing else.

Luce hadn't really considered the sleeping arrangements before now. The woman dropped two keys into Mat's hand and alerted them that room service was available until 10:00 p.m., then she was gone.

Luce placed her overnight bag down then sat on the bed, taking in the accommodations. "It's pretty," she offered.

He rubbed his hand over his short-cropped hair and looked around the small space. Luce could practically see the gears turning in his head. "I could probably sleep on the floor," he said.

She shrugged. "It's up to you. Whatever you feel most comfortable with." She picked up her bag and began unpacking.

"So, you don't care?" He spoke slowly, as if not believing her.

"It's a big bed, Mat. And we're grown-ups. We can tie a ribbon down the middle to keep our sides separate if you want." She forced a smile, trying to act as nonchalant as possible but the thought of sleeping next to him was giving her *feelings*.

He was wearing a plain, white T-shirt, dark jeans, and his trademark boots. Things were rippling in places where men should ripple, and she had to force herself to remember that this was all fake. He was a runner—off to the next city or country before she could blink an eye, and she was a stayer—solid, stable, steady.

That set her straight. She didn't need to settle. Just the fact that she was in this position at all was evidence that Mat and her weren't on the same page. She was doing him an enormous favor, in addition to helping out his delightful sister and earning a relaxing, free vacation…where she'd have to lie to everyone she met. No problem.

"So, what's our story? We should synchronize swatches, right?" she asked.

He looked at her blankly.

"No *Parker Lewis Can't Lose* reruns in East India? It means get our stories straight. Where was our first date?"

"Umm…" He frowned and looked away, thinking.

Luce stared. "Where would you take a girl on a first date?"

He was hesitant. "I don't really do a lot of dating."

"Oh," she said, understanding dawning. "So you just get straight to the fucking? Great."

"No, that's not what I mean. Not always. It's just—"

"No problem. I get it. Well, how about dinner? That's pretty safe and generic. We went to Biscuits and Blues and LaVay

Smith was performing. You like nouveau retro swing, right? We stayed for her second set and then went for ice cream after. Think you can remember that?"

Mat looked annoyed. "You don't have to manage everything, Luce."

"I don't? So you have this completely under control, right?" She crossed her arms, staring at him. His brow scrunched in a way that would be adorable, if it wasn't so infuriating.

"Yeah, that's what I thought." She pulled a change of clothes from her bag along with her toiletries kit. "I'm taking a shower. Curtain up in less than an hour."

Mat lay back on the bed staring at the ceiling. It was one of those textured ones with the waves plastered into them. He'd had a few like that as a kid and they always reminded him of bad times.

This was never going to work. Luce could barely even stand him. She was a planner and that wasn't his strong suit. Even though he wasn't as comfortable around people as she obviously was, he'd far prefer to just wing it, handle things as they came, and not blow things out of proportion.

He fished out the sketchbook from his backpack and started drawing. His hand moved across the page, calming him with each line. He wasn't conscious of, or intending to draw anything in particular, but soon he looked down into a pair of eyes staring back at him from an oval face. Luce's eyes, judgmental, assessing him and finding him lacking. He couldn't disagree.

What kind of man caused his sister to worry so much about him that she didn't even feel she could get married and live her dream? He slammed the sketchbook shut as Luce emerged from the bathroom.

He had to fight not to stare, but he lost. She was breathtaking. Wearing a strapless dress which skimmed the floor, the lines of her shoulders and collarbones were just begging to be kissed. Her skin was so damn soft. He wished he didn't remember how soft.

Another thing he couldn't seem to forget? How her body had felt pressed against his as he carried her to relative safety in the midst of the earthquake. She'd been light in his arms, but curvy. The sensation of silken, velvety skin against his fingertips made him stifle a moan.

His mouth was suddenly dry, and he couldn't tear his gaze away from her. The dress she wore was form fitting from chest to hips before flaring out all the way to the ground. Oranges and blues set off her skin tone perfectly. She looked like something he wanted to unwrap and spend all night licking.

Luce cleared her throat. He met her eyes and found her raising an eyebrow at him. He looked away quickly.

"You look nice," he said.

"Thanks. I'm not a huge fan of car trips, so it's good to feel clean and human again."

She rifled through her bag, shooting him glances every so often. His face had probably turned colors; he always had a hard time hiding his embarrassment. There wasn't much point in fantasizing about the way she'd felt in that storage room. How close they'd been huddled together for safety under a metal desk. Even in the crazy, dangerous circumstances, or maybe because of them, the feel of her had sealed itself in his memory.

He'd been hoping the hotel room would have a couch, or a chair. He would even consider sleeping in the bathroom, but there was only a stand-up shower. And the place was small enough that if he slept on the floor, she'd step on him if she needed to get up during the night.

He'd have to suck it up and push these feelings away, otherwise he was in for a very long weekend.

EIGHT

LUCE STOOD ALONG THE WALL, nursing the same flute of champagne that had been foisted upon her when she first entered the inn's small ballroom. Not far away, Mat was laughing with a group of hipster musician types. He looked over at her and she smiled brightly, lifting the glass in his direction to assuage the concern in his gaze.

She'd been engaged in conversation with Micah's mother for the past few minutes—a fascinating and intense woman who hadn't required another participant in her monologue. After nodding and making appropriate sounds of agreement and shock when needed, Luce was a bit relieved when the older woman walked off to ensure the hors d'oeuvres were being plated properly. She was happy to now take the opportunity to absorb the festivities.

Charlotte flounced around the room in a fluffy, pink dress, a huge smile on her face. She was naturally effervescent, and seeing her so happy helped to temper Luce's guilt about perpetuating this ridiculous lie.

Out on the terrace, a jazz quartet played up-tempo music. She wandered through the French doors to enjoy the crisp, fresh country air. This was her vacation and she was determined to enjoy it. That was, after all, her main reason for coming.

She felt a presence behind her and inhaled, taking in a warm, spicy scent. "Having a good time?" she asked, turning to face her date. In his slim-fitting suit, he was more gorgeous than ever. She ran through her checklist quickly, and rubbed her lips together, just to make sure her mouth stayed closed and no drool escaped.

His head tilted down, Mat looked at her from beneath his long fringe of eyelashes. "Yeah, are you?"

"It's beautiful here," she said, a little wistful. "And the party is lovely."

Silence stretched between them and Luce noticed that Mat wasn't looking her in the eye. "What's up?"

He scratched his head and twisted his lips. "Well, ah…"

She narrowed her eyes. "What happened?"

"So, I may have sort of agreed to play a game. I mean for us…together…to play a…sort of couples game."

"What kind of couples game?"

He turned his head to the side and squinted. "I'm not exactly sure. But Charlotte's really excited about it."

Luce's heart began to race. "This isn't the kind of game where we prove how much we know about each other, is it?"

He scratched his head again, eyes wide. "Maybe?"

"Are you insane?"

Mat blew out a breath. "It can't possibly be that bad. Trial by fire, right?"

Luce was sputtering and trying to come up with an answer to that inane statement, when he grabbed her hand and began tugging her back into the ballroom.

Her palms were sweating. She didn't want to get worked up for nothing, but she hated being unprepared. Thinking on the fly was not her strong suit. She needed preparation, practice, notes at the very least. Why hadn't they created dossiers for each other? That's what she really should have been doing on the drive up.

Her heart was now officially in the turbo zone. Mat must have noticed something wrong because he stopped in the middle of the room and turned to look at her, worry creasing his face.

"Luce—"

The ringing of a cowbell interrupted him. Someone had gotten the bright idea to play a modified version of the wedding reception game where when the bell went off, everyone who was there with a partner had to kiss. So far, Luce had managed to avoid it because she and Mat had separated almost as soon as they'd entered the party. But here they were, in the center of the ballroom, surrounded by several dozen people who were supposed to believe they were a couple.

All around them, pairs embraced and kissed. Luce's gaze skittered, hoping everyone else was too involved in themselves to notice what she and Mat were doing. But Mat must have seen something she missed. He pulled her flush against him and slanted his lips across hers.

The speedy flutter in her chest grew to a full thrashing. Her blood warmed as his tongue breached her lips. She wrapped an arm around his broad shoulders as he pulled her even closer until all she could feel was the hardness of his body against her.

He deepened the kiss, his hand lightly gripping the back of her head, and her memory blanked out. Her checklist, her guilt, her reservations—all dissolved. There was a very good reason they shouldn't be doing this, but for the life of her, she had no idea why. She would have been hard pressed to remember her phone number or birthday at this point.

The fantasies of Mat that had slipped past her mental barriers over the past weeks had nothing on this. She obviously was not a very good fantasizer because she'd failed miserably to capture how firm his lips were, exactly how good his smell would be this close, where every breath she took was full of him. The way he held her—firm but gentle. *Preciously*. She disappeared inside the kiss and almost didn't resurface.

Until he pulled back. Her instinct was to chase after him, insist they not stop, but her senses began to come back online one by one. Instead of smelling only him, the scents of food and wine returned. Sound was next—the band still played on the terrace, a classic Dave Brubeck tune.

Mat's dark amber eyes were wide, looking as shocked as she felt. She could see him shake it off, blink and then look around as if coming back to reality.

That's what she had to do as well. Shake it off.

She hoped he didn't feel the actual shaking in her hand when he gripped it again. Still firm and gentle. He intertwined their fingers together and led her through the ballroom to one of the smaller parlors in the inn.

The people they passed looked normal. None of them seemed to have gone through another 5.7 earthquake. Apparently, none of them had felt the ground-shaking ferocity of what she'd just experienced, and she had no idea what to do about it.

The sitting area had been turned into a game room with three tables set up. At one, a group of thirty-somethings were playing Settlers of Catan. Across the way, two older couples were locked in what appeared to be a contentious game of bid whist.

Luce smiled passing them. That was her parent's favorite and brought back some of the brighter memories from her childhood. In every city they'd lived, Moses and Joyce managed to befriend the black intelligencia and organized epic card parties full of smack talking and one-upmanship. It was at these parties where she'd first learned to play cards.

A third table had been set up in the back of the room. Charlotte and Micah stood next to it, and Luce was relieved to see Micah expertly riffle shuffling a deck of cards in mid-air.

"I thought we were in for some kind of newlywed game," Luce said, still cautious.

Eyes dancing, Charlotte motioned for them to sit. "I think spades is an excellent way to get to know each other."

"I like the way you think." Luce cracked her knuckles, feeling some residual effect of Charlotte's enthusiasm. She sat across from Mat at the folding table, taking in his lost expression. He actually looked a little green. "What's wrong?"

"I'm not that great a spades player," he admitted.

"Watch and learn, Mathias-san. I'm an excellent sensei."

They agreed on the rules after a brief disagreement on sandbagging penalties—Micah advocated a hardcore style of play where each sandbag was negative ten points, but he was voted down by everyone else.

"Let's just keep it simple this first round," Charlotte said, eyeing her brother warily. She dealt, and since Luce was on her left, she bid first.

"I've got four and a possible," she said. Mat pressed his lips together. Changed the order of his cards, then changed them back.

Charlotte bid three and then it was Mat's turn to say how many books he thought he could make with his hand. In spades, two players on a team worked together to win each hand—a book. Higher cards won the round, but spades were trumps, beating all others except the two jokers. Mat was her partner, and to win the game effective bidding, based on the cards in your hand you thought would win the round, was key.

"One," he said, then put his cards down.

Luce's brows rose. Maybe he just had a shit hand. But when Micah bid three, Luce did the math. There were thirteen possible books to be made. Assuming that Char and Micah knew what they were doing with their bidding and that her own possible became a reality, that left two books unaccounted for. It looked like Mat had underbid.

Sure enough, when the round ended, Mat had actually made

four books, negating not only her possible but two of Charlotte's assumed wins.

"You had three spades and a joker in that hand, Mat. Why would you only bid one book?" She tried to keep the exasperation from her voice.

"They were just so low," he said, shrugging. Luce took a deep breath. Usually with new players you had to worry about reneging—bidding too high and then not making the books. But Mat had the opposite problem, one she hadn't considered would be an issue for him.

She recalled Moses sitting down with her and explaining the rules of the game when she'd been about eight or nine. "The key to spades is confidence," he'd said. "Not just in yourself, but your partner. Over time you learn how to read each other. Learn *how* possible their possibles are and how they tend to bid. Good team work equals success."

Mat wasn't confident, at least not in his bidding. Now that she thought about it, though he appeared self-assured on the outside, he didn't seem to have a ton of faith in himself. He wasn't overly apologetic all the time like some, but his quiet manner seemed to hide a sense of unease.

When he presented designs at work, it wasn't with a flourish, but with the expectation that they would be unacceptable, and he'd have to go back to the drawing board. She hadn't thought much of it until now.

Luce dealt the next hand and kept this in mind as they bid again. This time, since he bid before her, she mentally added two to his low number, and adjusted her bidding accordingly.

"So, Mat," Micah said while waiting for Charlotte to take her turn, "are you thinking you might stick around a bit longer now that you're seeing Luce?"

Mat studied his hand intently, but Luce didn't miss the slight paling of his skin under his warm, golden tone. "Well, Luce hasn't done much traveling, so I think it would be great to show her some places she hasn't seen before."

Luce bristled. "My father is really sick, so I don't see being able to get away any time soon." Mat looked up, concern in his eyes that touched her even as his words had annoyed her.

"His COPD is pretty serious, and he hasn't been that great about taking care of himself," she admitted.

Charlotte nodded. "Yeah, that's tough. I understand why you have to stay close to home."

Mat shifted in his seat as if the very idea of staying close to home made him itchy. Luce buried the anger that sparked within her and focused on her cards. Her strategy was working; they'd made their bid and once again, Mat had made more books than he'd originally thought he could.

"How's your job going?" Char asked her brother.

"My contract was only two months, but our boss, Bobby, has already said he'd love for me to stay on."

Luce looked up, surprised. "I didn't know that."

"Yeah, he just told me this morning, actually." Mat's eyes locked onto hers sending a message she couldn't decipher.

"That's great news," Char said, triumphantly winning the book with a three of spades. "So you *might* stick around then."

Mat cleared his throat. "It would be nice to sleep in the same bed for a while. I actually like working there. It's different every day because of all the people around. Almost like not working in an office at all." The statement seemed to stun him, and Luce smothered a smirk.

"Yeah, it's not so bad," she said. "I do miss the info desk downstairs sometimes. The unwashed masses can be invigorating." They smiled at each other, then at the same moment seemed to catch themselves doing it and looked away.

"What would you do if you weren't doing...what is it that you do again, Luce?" Micah asked.

"I'm in PR. And I don't know. I worked at a tour company for a while in college. It's rough and more unpredictable than I wanted, but you get to move around a lot, talk to people from all over the world, and share the city with them. It's…rewarding in an unexpected way."

Mat was staring at her again. "I can see that. I think you'd be great as a tour guide."

Her cheeks felt warm at his praise.

"Luce has a real way with people," Mat said. "She can get them to open up to her and share things. It's pretty amazing." Was something wrong with her hearing or was that admiration in his voice?

Charlotte produced the coveted big joker, ending the round in her favor.

"Nice, baby," Micah said. They fist bumped over the table.

"You guys are a good team. Looks like engagement agrees with you." Luce was honestly happy for them, though as the love birds stared at each other sappily, a lump lodged in her throat. Must be nice.

Mat was busy tallying the score and looked up grinning. "We're tied, three games each."

Charlotte laughed. "That's more games than you've ever won in your life, Mat." She turned to Luce. "You're good for him."

"Want a tie breaker?" Mat asked.

Char sighed and shook her head. "I'd better get back out there. The good thing about this party is it's pretty low key, but I should do one more round of socializing."

"Thanks, this was really fun," Luce said, glad that she meant it.

Charlotte grabbed her hand and squeezed. "I'm really glad you could come. It's been so wonderful getting to know you." She looked like she would say more but Micah was behind her, pulling out her chair.

Luce's own chair moved, and she looked up to find Mat there, being very gentlemanly. He helped her up; her hand in his sizzled at the contact.

"Thank you." Her voice sounded breathless to her own ears. She hoped Mat didn't hear it.

Now that they were standing side by side, her gaze once again drifted to his lips, her mind replaying their earlier kiss. That was against the rules; it could lead to other unwanted reactions, but she couldn't seem to look away. An electric charge built up between them, crackling with energy.

The room fell away. Charlotte said something but she couldn't hear it. Mat leaned closer. Was he going to kiss her again? She wouldn't mind even if there was no bell. That would really sell this whole charade, wouldn't it?

His scent filled her nostrils and she pressed her thighs together. What would it be like to—

When Charlotte spoke again, the sheer horror lacing her voice cut through the haze. Mat heard it too and pulled away. His expression transformed from wondrous to dismayed. "Shit."

Luce turned to see what caused the reaction.

An older, ebony complexioned man stood in the entry to the inn's lobby. Charlotte and Mat were both frozen in place, identical looks of chagrin on their faces.

Luce took his hand and squeezed. "What's the matter? Who's that?"

Mat's voice was empty, with just a hint of anger. "Our dad."

NINE

THE UPBEAT MUSIC filtering in from outside became a drone in Mat's ear. It buzzed like a wasp burrowing under his skin. The sharp pain welling inside him was almost as intense.

The Colonel strode through the foyer wearing a black suit with wide lapels. His dark clothes and darker expression made it look like he was going to a funeral. Mat hadn't seen him in years. The man's hair was receding, though he still kept it cropped brutally short. His face was weathered. He was beginning to look old.

Reflexively, Mat straightened his spine and pushed his shoulders back, adopting a more acceptable posture, then inwardly chastised himself for doing so. It was second nature around his father, though. He didn't want to take his eyes off the man, but he had to see how Charlotte was faring. She looked as shocked as he felt, which answered the question of whether she had invited him.

"Dad, what are you doing here?" Her voice was shaky. Mat wanted to throttle the interloper for disturbing his sister's celebration. She moved forward to meet him with Mat on her heels.

Micah and Luce were there as well, forming a network of support he wasn't used to.

The Colonel looked around, taking in every detail of his surroundings. A few of the guests had stopped, apparently noticing the tension. But most were still oblivious—in the ballroom dancing or gathered in other areas of the inn drinking and eating. At least the entire party wasn't ruined.

Yet.

"So, you're getting married, Charlotte?" Faint hints of his Jamaican accent were still audible in his clipped speech. But the sound of his voice after so many years made something inside of Mat crack a little. He took a deep breath for strength.

Charlotte blinked, looking lost, then Micah took her hand, visibly shoring up her strength.

"Yes, Dad, this is Micah, my fiancé. Micah my father, Colonel Lennox Woodson."

Micah and the Colonel shook hands.

"Customary for a potential groom to ask the father's permission first, is it not?" The Colonel's smirk held no mirth.

Micah didn't miss a beat. "Dowries and arranged marriages are also customary in some places. Just not twenty-first century America, sir." His voice was respectful, but firm. The Colonel sniffed, dismissing the younger man.

Mat's father's gaze then landed on him before moving to Luce. An almost imperceptible raise of his eyebrows was all the reaction the man gave.

"A-and this is Mat's girlfriend, Luce," Charlotte said.

"Lucinda Garvey." Luce extended her hand. Mat knew how forceful his father's handshakes were and that he didn't take gender or bone size into consideration. But Luce looked like she gave as good as she got; the muscles in her forearm tensed as she squeezed back. Some empty part of his heart filled upon seeing it.

"Garvey. Where are your people from?" the Colonel asked.

Luce smiled. "No relation to Marcus, I'm afraid. My father's from Alabama. Fayette, originally."

The Colonel sniffed. "Slave stock," he muttered.

Mat could feel Luce tense. "Dad—" he began.

But Luce cut him off. "Oh, so your ancestors sailed from Africa to Jamaica voluntarily? Fascinating."

The Colonel bristled. "My people were maroons. They escaped slavery and fought back against the European oppressors."

"So, they *were* slaves, at one point?" Luce's chin jutted out proudly. "I'm not ashamed of that. My ancestors built this country. America would never have become what it is without our blood and sweat in the soil."

Mat could see the veins in his father's forehead pulse. Though the Colonel had lived in the States for decades and gained his citizenship, he had a low opinion of black Americans and never failed to share that with whomever he was around.

Instead of responding to Luce, Mat's father sniffed again and turned away, indicating the conversation was over. Charlotte and Micah stood looking at Luce with awe.

"How did you know about the party?" Mat asked through gritted teeth.

"Facebook," the Colonel replied.

Charlotte shot Mat a questioning glance. "You're on Facebook, Dad?"

"No. Of course not. But I know people who are. I assume my invitation was lost in the mail." His brows rose. "I think I'll take a look around the festivities." He executed an about-face and marched off into the ballroom.

Charlotte was aghast. There was a reason that neither had seen the man in years and that he hadn't been invited in the first place. It wasn't just because he was overly strict, mean as a snake, and lacked the gene for love. No, he was also a rude bastard who bulldozed his way through every interaction with other human beings.

Growing up, he'd taught his two children that they were superior to all others and they didn't need anyone else. The Colonel hadn't blinked when his wife abandoned him and their children. He'd expected them to pick up and go on like nothing had happened. He threw himself into his work, advancing steadily, moving regularly, and leaving everything else, including his children, behind.

"I'm so sorry for him," Charlotte was saying to Luce and Micah.

Luce held her hand up. "No need. We can't choose our parents. I understand that more than most."

Charlotte nodded and looked worriedly in the direction he'd gone.

"Let me go talk to him," Mat said, though the idea caused rivulets of sweat to run down his back. They were the same height now, he wasn't a little boy anymore, and he doubted his father would become violent, but still the cold fear gripped him. The fear he'd never been able to shake. He still ran from it.

But now he stalked after the man, through the path of bewildered partygoers left in his wake because the Colonel stopped for no one. He found him at the bar in the corner of the room, throwing back a Jack and Coke. A drink sounded like an excellent idea right about now.

"Moscow mule," Mat said to the bartender.

The Colonel snorted. "You drink like a girl. If you want vodka, ask for vodka."

"I ordered what I wanted." Mat paused and took a deep breath. "And my girlfriend doesn't seem to have a problem with it." He wasn't sure why he added the last part; what did he care what his father thought of his masculinity?

"Ah, why are you with that gal? She's a bit dark, don't you think?" Ironic because she and the Colonel were about the same complexion. But his father had always liked them blonde, a predilection Mat didn't share.

He wouldn't allow the man to disparage Luce any further.

"Don't speak about her. Just keep her name off your lips. Why did you come, really?" He took a sip of his drink and relished the burn as it went down. It matched the fire already in his belly and gave a shot of courage he desperately needed.

"Why shouldn't I be here? My oldest daughter is getting married. To a man without a real job no less." He shook his head and slammed his empty glass on the counter, demanding a refill.

"Micah has a job. He's a musician. In a successful band."

"Musicians." He waved his hand dismissively. "That kind of success is here one day and gone the next. At any rate, I'm your father, and I have a right to be here."

Mat's hackles rose. "What rights you had you gave up when you abandoned us."

"Abandoned?" His voice surged, causing others nearby to turn and stare. "Who put food on the table? Kept a roof over your heads? Me. I did all of it, and I got no thanks."

"You want thanks?" Mat asked, anger growing. "Is that what you came here for? For us to genuflect on our knees with gratitude at how great it was to have an empty home to come back to? The wonderful experience of forging our names on papers for school because you were never home? To be appreciative of how Charlotte had to put off college to take care of me because you couldn't be bothered? Well, thanks, Dad."

The Colonel was seething, eyes loaded with ammunition and ready to fire. "I was a man, and I handled my responsibilities. What are you? Running around the globe with no place to call home. When I traveled, it was for a purpose. I was protecting this country and my family so you could have the luxury to make drawings for a living."

"I am a graphic designer," Mat growled. "And I live my life the way I choose. *I* don't hurt anyone with *my* actions."

"Pshaw. You're a little boy still crying about how Daddy didn't love him enough. Running away from any sense of accountability. When I was your age, I had real duties, people depending on me. What do you have? Who are you to question me? When you grow up and become a man, then talk to me about my choices."

With that, his father took his drink and walked off onto the terrace. Mat was left standing there reeling. His fists tightening as rage blinded his vision.

Toxic. His father had always been toxic. With a fast and poisonous tongue. Part of Mat wanted to storm after the man. Part of him wanted to shrivel into a ball and never emerge. A warm hand on his made him look up.

Luce stood there, focused intently on him. How much had she heard? Enough that her eyes were filled with emotion. Inside him was turmoil, a raging sea of guilt and pain, dredging up detritus from the bottom.

"Come with me," she said, gently uncurling his fingers and taking his hand in hers. She led him away this time, to where, he didn't care.

TEN

LUCE GUIDED Mat onto the dance floor. The band had stopped playing outside and a DJ had taken up the slack. Couples were swaying to the soothing tones of a love song, one of Toni Braxton's, sung low and sad.

She wrapped her arms around him and pulled him close. They were near the spot where they shared their first kiss only a few hours ago, but it could have been a lifetime.

Mat was stiff in her arms. But she didn't let it bother her. She kept hold of him and swayed gently, not even really trying to dance. She suspected he just needed positive human contact. Talking would come, *if* he would confide in her. But for now, movement. Touch. A reminder that everyone wasn't that awful man he had for a father.

She felt sorry for Charlotte and Mat. While her parents were no prize—selfish and neglectful and quick with cutting words— she'd never experienced anything quite like what she'd over- heard Mat's father say to him. She vowed to be more grateful about what she did have. You never knew someone's story until you walked a mile in their shoes.

Eventually, Mat's rigid limbs loosened. He tightened his hold on her and then they were really dancing. Nothing fancy, still mostly swaying back and forth but with purpose. She wasn't just holding him up to keep him from falling over anymore. His heart thrummed in his chest, and she felt it in her sternum.

Telling herself it was for the sake of the other guests and the ongoing deception, she leaned her head on his shoulder and exhaled. If she could pull his pain into her, she would. That thought startled her, making her peer a little more deeply into her feelings. He was a good man, he didn't deserve the pain, that was all.

When the song ended and changed to the upbeat "Cha Cha Slide," Luce thought he'd want to leave the dance floor. But to her surprise, a tiny smile lit his face. Who didn't like the "Cha Cha Slide"?

The line dance drew the majority of the guests to the dance floor to take part in the easy steps directed by the voice on the track. They slid and criss-crossed their legs and jumped up and down together. The vibe was light and fun.

She spied Charlotte and Micah taking part as well and her blood pumped a little at the joy catching through the small crowd. The party wasn't ruined, not quite. Thankfully, their father was nowhere in sight.

She and Mat stayed on the dance floor through the next few songs. Luce kicked her shoes off when the DJ really started playing the hits. They danced and laughed, worries forgotten for the moment. She knew it was just a calm between storms, but she was still grateful for it. Grateful too for Mat's resilience, another good quality in him she had to admire. Finally, she begged off the dance floor, too tired to shake her ass anymore. Mat snagged a bottle of champagne and they walked hand in hand to the terrace.

Everything was winding down, though a few tables were still occupied by stragglers. Wordlessly they agreed to settle at a picnic table on the grass just beyond the covered terrace. The night was lovely but getting cooler.

"Want my jacket?" Mat offered.

Her lips were forming a refusal when Mat draped his jacket around her shoulders. It was warm with his body heat. She didn't want to sniff his scent embedded in the fabric but couldn't help herself. They sat side by side on the wooden bench, passing the bottle back and forth between them.

"Do you…want to talk about it?" she asked, taking a swig of fizzy champagne.

He leaned back, tilting his head to the star-laden sky. The column of his throat held her attention, strong and solid, as she waited for him to reply.

"I just didn't want him to ruin her day. Her weekend. He has that unique capacity."

Luce chuckled. "Yeah, I kind of got that."

Mat shook himself and turned to her, the lantern making his eyes glow. There was tenderness there, or was she imagining it?

"So how do you think it went?" she asked, trying to bring some clarity to her mind.

A real smile broke through on his face. "Pretty good. I think we pulled it off. Were our swatches synchronized enough for you?"

She shrugged. "I guess so. Charlotte didn't seem suspicious?"

"I don't think so. She likes you." His smile dropped. "She really likes you."

"I like her too. She's great. I'm so happy for her." Luce played with the label, peeling off little strips and then flicking them away.

She took a deep breath. The idea had come to her suddenly, and though she wasn't sure it was a good one, the words slipped from her mouth. "Do you think…when we get back that is, maybe we could…I don't know, go out for real?"

She held her breath and stared at her fingers. As the silence stretched out longer, she looked over at him. That same tenderness was in his eyes, but they were also sad. And she knew the answer.

"Never mind."

"No, I—I just, wouldn't be good for you."

She quirked an eyebrow. Mat straightened up and loosened his collar. "I'm not good at relationships. I don't have the best role models and I'm just not..." He trailed off and slumped down a little. "Besides, I thought I was an overgrown child."

She stiffened, but there was no anger in his words. He stared at his splayed hands.

"I think you're pretty grown up," she said. "For the most part."

"Responsibility's not exactly my thing, you know."

"You take care of Charlotte. I know that you went to talk to your father just to keep her happy."

He shook his head. "Yeah, but that's not the same thing. I'll be leaving eventually. She'll be gone soon. And she's got Micah. It's all...it'll be the way it's supposed to be." But he sounded dejected, and Luce wasn't sure he believed his words.

At any rate, she'd taken her shot and been shot down. She stood and brushed off her dress. "Maybe you're right. I'm going to bed. See you later."

She crossed the yard quickly, heading back inside.

"Luce, wait."

She paused on the steps, but didn't turn around. The quiet night stretched out behind her, fields of grapes filling the air with their heady scent. As the silence stretched on, her heart shuddered.

Mat was kind and caring. Sweet and talented. And she liked him, a lot. More than she wanted to, that's for sure. She liked the way he protected his sister. She liked the way he cared so much.

But he didn't care for her. And that was the thing really. This was all still fake. So she would suck it up and enjoy the rest of her weekend, then go back to reality.

She crossed the threshold and disappeared into the inn,

leaving him outside on the terrace, along with whatever it was he couldn't say.

Shit. He'd frozen and hadn't meant to. He jumped up and followed her back into the building. But Luce was moving quickly and though her legs were shorter than his, he didn't catch up until they were in the upstairs hallway near their room.

"Luce."

She kept going, sticking her key in the lock and turning. He followed into the small guest room where there was nowhere to hide. She moved to the other side of the bed and sat down facing away from him. "It's fine, really," she said. "Stupid idea." Her shoulders rose, and Mat felt gutted.

"Not a stupid idea. Not at all. It...it makes sense."

She snorted. "How?"

He paced over to sit next to her. She didn't look at him, staring resolutely at the wall in front of her, body stiff.

"I just think you could do better."

She raised her brows skeptically.

"I'm serious," he said.

"Whatever."

"Luce."

She pivoted sharply toward him and a whiff of her scent assaulted him. Her gaze was wary, waiting for his excuse.

He dredged his mind for the ones he usually used when he thought things were getting too serious. He was broke. He was leaving. He didn't do relationships. But they wouldn't come out of his mouth.

The moment stretched on, and her wariness grew. The only thing he could really think about was how good she smelled. How nice it had felt to hold her and dance with her. How much fun they'd had.

How, when he first started working at the Button Factory

and had met her, they'd shaken hands. His palm had stung. He'd ignored it.

He couldn't ignore it any more.

His hand rose to cup her face. She looked as surprised as he felt. Her gaze dropped to his lips then skittered away, but he wanted it back.

The memory of their kiss rushed at him, reanimating his frozen limbs. He leaned forward, expecting her to stop him, but she didn't. She closed her eyes, and he was gone. Lost when their lips pressed together, once again drowning in her essence. He couldn't get enough. The eagerness with which she clung to him spurred him on. The space between them disappeared as he dragged her forward onto his lap.

Need and desire fused as he tilted his head and she began to devour him. He didn't have to think about it or rationalize it. Or worry there would be expectations. He was in the present moment diving in head first. Breathing her in like a man trapped underground experiencing fresh air again.

On a gasp, they tore apart. He wasn't sure what would happen next, but recognized calculation in her eyes. Doubt, then resolve.

"Do you have condoms?" she asked.

He swallowed. Nodded. "Are you…are you sure?"

She paused, and he held his breath. Not wanting to push her in any way.

Luce smiled a devilish smile he'd never seen on her before, slid off him, and reached behind her to unzip her dress. His mouth went dry when the colorful fabric dropped away, revealing a strapless bra and thong.

She looked down at his fully clothed chest significantly. "Your turn."

He removed his already loosened tie and started on the buttons to his shirt, fumbling briefly when Luce took off her bra. Impatient, she pushed his fingers out of the way and from then on, it seemed like it was a race. Their remaining clothes practically evaporated; the heat coming off their bodies was intense.

Luce took charge in her no-nonsense way, which he appreciated now. Her hands slid over his chest and arms reverently. Then they glided lower, below his waist, stroking him. Applying a firm pressure; caressing and gripping harder until he had to stop her or this would be over quickly.

He needed time for this. He'd wanted to feast on her skin for so long and wasn't about to lose his opportunity due to any premature outbursts. Taking the reins, he flipped them so he was on top and tasted her from neck to navel, delighting in her cries of pleasure. Then he delved lower.

Spreading her wide, he positioned her thighs on his shoulders and focused on making her scream. She was quiet at first, then scrabbled for purchase, trying in vain to pull his short hair. She settled for squeezing his head. It didn't hurt, instead made him chuckle as he lapped up her juices. Finally, a scream tore through her—wrenched from her body into the air to thrill his ears.

Satisfied, he crawled up her limp form and reached for the condom in his wallet.

Her droopy eyes widened as he sheathed himself. She quickly rallied, spreading her legs wider to accommodate the width of his body as he settled in.

Their gazes met, hers glittering, sparking with excitement, which he fed off. He took in every small reaction as his length nudged her entrance. Her gasp when he first pushed inside. The "o" formed by her lips as he slid smoothly into her heat.

Then he had to close his eyes to settle himself as he sunk in deeper. A ragged breath betrayed the effort he was expending holding still, allowing her to adjust to him.

After a prod from her, which took the form of her clamping down on him, he began to move, retreating before pumping in farther, coaxing out cries that spurred him on. Relishing the bite of her nails on his back and his ass. He was fully lost in her, and she grew wild beneath him. Biting her lip in an effort not to shout.

"Let go," he whispered like an incantation. Maybe these old walls were thin, but he really didn't care. She obliged with moans and cries of pleasure as he moved inside her.

All he knew was Luce, her scent, her warmth, the tight grip she held him in, and the wonder of reaching release in her arms.

Sweating and heaving breaths, he collapsed next to her, arms and legs still tangled. Soon he would get up and dispose of the condom, but for now he wanted another moment of bliss. Another moment in her embrace.

ELEVEN

SATURDAY'S neatly-printed schedule included brunch, a vine-yard tour, a series of games that reminded Mat of field day in elementary school, followed by dinner, and then casino night. But what he really wanted to do was stay in bed all day. He suggested as much to Luce who just laughed before bouncing up, bright as anything, to hit the shower.

Oh no, she's a morning person.

Mat turned over and went back to sleep. Only to be awoken by Luce's sing-song voice taunting him about missing brunch and being hungry all day. She did have a point. He reluctantly rose, then got a good look at the sundress she was wearing. Which accentuated her curves in a way he wasn't ready for at this hour of the morning.

He grabbed her in a bear hug and wrestled her squealing form back on the bed.

"Oh, no you don't," she said, laughing. "My hangriness is legendary, and I don't think you're ready to experience all of that yet."

She wiggled out of his grip to stand, straightening her dress.

"Get up, I'll save you something tasty." And with a wink, she was gone.

Twenty minutes later, he was shoving food in his mouth, glad he'd listened to her. They'd worked up quite the appetite the night before, and he did need his strength. They sat at a table with some of Micah's cousins, one of whom, a pretty-boy stockbroker with a laser cut fade, was paying close attention to Luce. A little too close for his liking. Mat draped a possessive arm around her while she regaled them with a story about her days as a tour guide and an incident involving a runaway baby carriage —empty, thankfully—on the crookedest street in the world.

He felt his jealousy fracture when she nestled deeper into his side. They were just finishing up their meal when Luce's phone buzzed in her purse. She ignored it, but when it started vibrating again, she sighed and pulled it out.

When her face went ashen, Mat sat up straighter. "What's wrong?"

"It's Delilah." Her voice was cautious as she answered the call. "Hey, what's up? Okay, slow down. Which hospital did they take him to?"

Mat's heart seized.

She blew out a breath. "I left the name of his doctor with the other info. Can you call him? And the insurance information is —okay, right. Yeah."

Luce looked up at him with sad eyes. "No, thank you so much. I'll be back as soon as I can. Hopefully, there's no traffic."

She ended the call and pursed her lips. "It's my dad. He's in the hospital."

"I'm so sorry, Luce." He ran a hand up and down her arm trying to think of what he could do to help.

"I-I need to go back." She looked up at him with shining eyes.

"Right, of course."

An unspoken question hung in her gaze. He should go back

with her, make sure everything was all right. The air in the dining room seemed to crackle with electric energy. Everyone looked up at the same time to find the Colonel standing at the threshold, looking around imperiously. A knot, cold and painful, twisted inside of Mat.

What good would he do if he went with Luce? She had her friend, Delilah. He'd probably just be in the way. It's not like he could really do anything.

She might appreciate having you there, a voice whispered in his mind. But he pushed the thought away.

Instead, he dug the keys to the rental car out of his pocket. "Take the car. I'll find another way back."

She stared at him, eyes large and round. The moment hung and his heart sank. Then she blinked and took a deep breath. "All right. I'd better go get my stuff. Please tell Charlotte I'm sorry I had to leave early, and that it was a lovely party."

He nodded and watched her leave without turning back once. Her shoulders were straight, her head high. A pit opened up inside of him, sucking him down into it.

He needed to get out of here. Not just the vineyard but the state. The country. He needed to book a flight somewhere. Someplace warm, maybe Costa Rica. His contract wasn't up at the Button Factory, but he could probably finish remotely.

After the party, Charlotte would get married and go on tour and there was no reason to stay anymore. He would go. And not think about what he was leaving behind.

The tour guide at the front of the bus droned on and on about the grapes and the wine and the growing conditions. Mat was sure Luce would have done a better job of making soil acidity sound interesting. However, even with slightly glazed expressions the rest of the guests at least looked like they were having a good time.

Mat sat in the back, sprawled across two seats, scrolling through his Facebook feed. Well, not his feed. The feed of the fake identity he'd set up years ago for one purpose—to friend his mother.

His fake name was Sigurd Hart, who also happened to be a Norwegian folk hero. Mat had purchased a stock photo of a smiling blonde haired, blue-eyed skier for his profile pic. Mom had accepted his friend request without incident, and he'd been cyber stalking her ever since.

Over the years, he'd learned of the births of his half-sisters and brother—siblings he'd never met. Saw them learn to crawl and walk and go to school. Family vacations, birthdays, holidays. Things that hadn't existed in the same way for a motherless boy.

When he wanted to torture himself, like now, he did so by watching his mother's life unfold with her perfect blonde family. Had that been the problem? Raising two black children was too difficult for her?

As if on cue, his father's voice rose from the front of the bus as he harangued the tour guide. "Why don't you just shut up for a moment and let us enjoy the scenery?"

The poor guide, a middle aged South Asian woman, froze, her mouth hanging open.

A tense silence took over before Micah's mother spoke up. "I was enjoying the information. I have a pair of headphones if you'd like to borrow them." She motioned the guide to continue. The woman did, though quite a bit more nervously than before.

Mat shook his head and closed the app. Who in their right mind would want to stay married to the Colonel? Mom had most likely been saving her sanity by leaving. But why hadn't she taken her children with her?

His body felt sluggish and dull. He might never know the answer.

A movement to his side startled him. A young woman with purple dreadlocks sat directly across the row from him.

"Delilah?" He looked around, confused. "How did you—where did you come from?"

She had not been sitting there a moment ago. She hadn't even gotten on the bus or been at the inn in the first place. Delilah shrugged and flipped a chunk of her bright hair, causing the bells weaved into her locs to jingle. The scent of incense wafted off her skin when she moved. "Bus transfer," she said with all seriousness.

Mat's mouth gaped open.

"Or temporal transference?" She scrunched her face in thought. "Wait, what do you all call it, wibbeldy wobbeldy…? But not time…space. *Spacial* transference. Getting onto a vehicle moving this quickly can be tricky, but I just got an upgrade to my system." She held up a digital tablet. The device was black and shiny, which should have been normal enough; however, for some reason hers looked weird. It had a few too many edges or something; Mat couldn't quite put his finger on it.

"Anyhoo," she said. "Why are you back here pouting?"

"I'm not pouting. And I still don't understand what you're doing here."

"I'm trying to save this assignment." She took a deep breath and leaned across the aisle toward him. "Listen, you don't want to be here do you?"

Mat squinted. "Here as in my sister's engagement weekend?"

She rolled her eyes. "Here as in without Luce-inda."

His face burned. "I would just get in her way. She needs to be with her family now. It didn't seem right for me to barge in."

"Barge in? You don't think that maybe having someone at her side right now would be helpful?"

"I kinda thought you would be there."

"Oh, I am. But this isn't about me, this is about you and your feelings of inadequacy."

He stiffened. "I don't feel inadequate."

Delilah raised an eyebrow and looked down at the darkened

phone in his hand significantly, as if she knew what he'd just been doing.

Mat deflated. "Trust me, Luce is better off without me. She's got real shit to deal with. Besides, I'm leaving at the end of the month."

"Even though Bobby asked you to stay?" She blinked her eyes, innocently.

"How did you know about that?" His brain hurt. None of this made any sense.

Up front, the Colonel's voice rose again. No doubt being a rude bastard, as usual. The tension in the air was thick; how did he worm his way onto this tour anyway? Who was paying for all these extra people who'd popped up?

Mat turned back to Delilah, but she was gone. Vanished into thin air with the scent of incense softly echoing in her wake.

TWELVE

THE REST of the weekend flew by as Mat went through the motions. He avoided his sister as much as possible and skipped out on the last few events to stew in his room. Laying on sheets that still smelled like Luce.

Sunday morning came and he was one of the first to check out and leave, getting a ride back to the city with Micah's pretty-boy stockbroker cousin, who was actually a hella decent dude.

During the ride back, he texted Luce for an update on her dad.

Luce: Still alive. For now. 👍 **(Brown thumbs up emoji)**

He'd sent back a smiley face after deleting the heart he'd origi-nally typed, then called himself all sorts of idiots for the rest of the day when she didn't text back. What did he expect?

Monday morning rolled around, and he was in the office early. Exactly why, he didn't know. He went in through the back entrance, which led directly to the offices, and stopped in front of Luce's darkened office to stare at the closed door.

She wouldn't be in today. He had no idea when he'd talk to her again; the uncertainty assaulted at him with its wrongness. He'd messed up. He knew that but had no idea what to do about it.

With a last look of regret, he headed toward the rows of cubicles where his desk was located. Then he stopped short.

"What is it with family members showing up at my job?" he muttered.

The Colonel stood there, glaring at Mina, the receptionist. Mat sized up the situation immediately—Mina had a tendency to flirt with just about everyone and seemed like the type of woman who was used to a warm reception. Only now she looked flustered and unaccustomed to the scowl pointed her way. When she saw Mat coming, her smile returned.

"Here he is!" she exclaimed brightly, motioning to him. "Mat, you have a visitor!" Then she took off toward her desk at a near run, impressive in her towering stilettos.

"Dad." Mat put his bag down on his desk and turned to face the Colonel.

"So, this is your latest job. Why don't you have an office, son?"

Mat took a deep breath. "Are you dying or something?"

His father's eyes went wide. "Why would you ask me that?"

"First you show up at Charlotte's party then here—when we haven't seen you in years. Something must be up, and I don't understand what it is."

The Colonel's back was as straight as ever, and Mat couldn't tell what, if any, emotion he was harboring inside his armor. "I'm retired now."

After a pause Mat said, "Congratulations?"

"There was a party and everything. Forty years in the service and now it's over." The man looked down, perhaps to hide the brief display of emotion on his face. It had looked something like vulnerability.

"At the party, everyone asked where my family was. It was…noticeable."

Mat wanted to feel some sense of compassion or pity, but it simply wasn't there. "You should have told them you don't have a family."

His father's head snapped up, gaze sharpened. "But I do. I brought two children into this world, clothed and fed them and kept a roof over their heads."

"Thank you for not letting me die, Dad. Now I have to get to work." Mat turned back toward his computer.

"You know what your problem is, boy?"

"No, please, tell me what is my problem?"

"You don't take anything seriously. You flit through the world with no reason for being, not caring about anyone but yourself."

The words hit home, and he couldn't even argue with them. Wasn't that what he'd done for years? Isn't that why he wasn't at the hospital with Luce right now? His shoulders slumped under the weight of his father's disregard.

"With all due respect," a voice rang out behind him, "you, sir, are full of shit."

Mat spun around to find Luce there, with heavy bags under her eyes, but still gorgeous in her yoga pants and an oversized sweatshirt.

The Colonel sputtered but Luce charged on. "Mat is extremely caring and generous. He helps people in need, plus he's solicitous of his sister's well-being to the point of absurdity." She sighed deeply, obviously exhausted, but fierce. "And he's a good man. Kind and talented and giving. I don't think he has you to thank for that. So if you came here to berate him, you should leave right now. But I suspect you came for something else?"

The Colonel glared down at her and Luce glared right back,

not giving an inch. Mat's already high respect for her increased —few could withstand the force of the Colonel's legendary disapproval. Mat himself had been running from it for years.

Luce crossed her arms.

"How's your dad?" Mat asked her.

She broke off the staring contest to look at him for the first time since she'd arrived. He drank her in, taking in every detail.

"He should be released tomorrow. I'm just here because I left my laptop over the weekend. Needed to get it so I can work from home this week. If I ever get home that is." A humorless chuckle escaped her. "At some point I need to get over there and make the place livable for him." She shook her head, obviously considering that a momentous task.

"He'll be bedridden for a while, and they need a hospital bed delivered, and food stocked, and a thousand other things." She took a deep breath and squared her shoulders. "But you eat an elephant one bite at a time, right?"

Mat wanted to go to her and pull her into his arms and tell her that it would be okay. Her adamant words to his father echoed in his head. Did she really believe those things about him? The Colonel was still there, looking at her with barely-contained ire. Luce ignored him, gave Mat a sad little wave before turning on her heel and leaving.

When she was gone, the air in the room seemed to have changed. What before had felt oppressive, was now lighter. Mat felt a shot of adrenaline that caused him to round on his father.

"You may not have abandoned us the way that Mom did, but you still left us. You left Charlotte to do the heavy lifting and never once apologized. She made sacrifices. We both felt it. So if there was no one at your retirement party, then the only person you have to blame is yourself. You're a toxic person to us and that's why we cut you out of our lives."

The Colonel began to speak, but Mat held up a hand to stop him. "But if Luce was right, and your presence here means that you're ready to start over, then the first thing you need to do is stop blaming us for your mistakes. And apologize. Is that something you can do?"

His father stared at him for a long time, his mouth working silently. His nostrils flared, and Mat could see the anger building. But instead of the explosion that he expected, the Colonel remained quiet. He pursed his lips and then left without saying another word.

Mat breathed in deeply and fell back into his chair. He'd never imagined saying anything like that to his father. Maybe one day their relationship would change and maybe it wouldn't—only time would tell. But Luce was probably right. The very fact that he'd backed down just now was the first sign. Mat had never known the man to leave an argument without having the last word.

The Colonel had work to do on himself, but then they all did. Mat was no exception. Maybe one day he could forgive. The future seemed so much more unknowable than he'd ever thought before.

He stared at the darkened monitor in front of him, fingers drumming on the desk. Then he picked up his bag and left his cubicle, headed for the front entrance of the office.

Mina sat at the reception desk, tapping on her phone.

"I need to take a personal day," he told her. "Family emergency."

"Oh, I hope everything is okay." She pouted with concern and blinked up at him.

"It's fine." He was all set to ignore her flirting the way he always had, but something made him stop at the door and turn back.

"I just need to go help my girlfriend with some stuff." He shrugged and pushed through the door, leaving her gaping at him.

THIRTEEN

LUCE TRUDGED down the sidewalk from the bus stop, exhaustion blurring her vision. She couldn't think straight and didn't know how she was going to handle the endless mountain of work facing her at her parents' apartment.

Moses would be released the next morning, bringing with him a host of instructions and requirements for his safety and well-being. There was no way he would be able to recover in his home the way it had been when she'd last seen it.

Thankfully, the fumigation was complete. She hoped she didn't find little roach carcasses everywhere. She shivered at the thought.

At the door, she closed her eyes, her mind once again returning to the past weekend and her abbreviated vacation. She breathed deeply, remembering the serenity. Recalling Mat's arms around her, the delicious way he smelled. The sensation of his fingers moving across her skin. The shiver running through her had a different quality now.

It was a new checklist, one that she'd used over the past two days to calm herself. And remind herself of what was possible. Even if it was all over now.

Reality had to come sooner or later. Probably best that she hadn't lived in fantasyland for too long. She opened her eyes and steeled her nerves before entering the duplex.

But her nerves took off at a gallop when she found the door to her parents' place ajar. She approached slowly, and pushed it open, thinking it must be the landlord, but not ruling out burglars. Though really, what was there to steal inside of Moses and Joyce's place?

"Hello?" she called out, then froze in place. If this was a robbery, they'd certainly been thorough.

The entire apartment had been transformed. Piles, boxes, crates, bags of God knew what were all gone. She could see the floor, and the furniture, and a coffee table she'd forgotten existed sparkled with furniture wax.

"What the hell happened?" she whispered.

From the kitchen, footsteps emerged. She no longer cared if thieves had stolen everything, they were welcome to it all. But instead of some criminal, Mat's smiling face greeted her. Something opened up inside Luce's chest. "Mat?" His grin was ear to ear as he took in her dazed expression. "What are you doing here?"

He was wearing the gray button-down he'd had on earlier, but his sleeves were rolled up and the top few buttons were undone. "I thought you could use some help. I got rid of all the junk in here, and the hospital bed is being delivered in about an hour. Along with a fresh oxygen tank and a filter for the AC system. It should help your father breathe easier even when he's not wearing the mask."

Luce struggled for words. "How did you do all of this?"

"Well, I had some help," he said. Charlotte, Micah, and Delilah appeared from around the corner.

"We're tackling the kitchen now," Charlotte said. "I hope you don't mind."

Luce shook her head. "No, I—I don't know what to say. Thank you...thank you all so much."

She'd waged a battle for years on this place, but never had the energy to do more than make it livable. What these four had done in a few hours was amazing. Beyond her wildest dreams. Tears pricked her eyes.

The others disappeared again, and Mat drew nearer, though still an arm's length away. He looked cautious. "I'm sorry I wasn't there for you earlier. I didn't…" He cleared his throat. "I wasn't sure that I could be the type of person you needed. I didn't really think I had anything to offer. But after what you said to my father this morning, I knew that I had to do something."

"Something," Luce said with a chuckle. "You did a hell of a lot more than something."

She couldn't stop the tears from streaming. Mat took a step closer and reached out to catch one. Luce shivered at his touch.

"What does this mean?" she whispered. "A good deed before you head off for parts unknown?"

He looked away and her heart sank. Some little part of her had hoped that perhaps this meant something more. "Yeah, about that," he said.

She shook her head and sniffed. "No, don't worry about it. It doesn't matter. I really appreciate everything you've done here. It means so much."

She went to move away, but he grasped her hands. "No, you don't understand. I decided to stay on longer. I want to stay."

She looked at him as if for the first time, swallowing the lump in her throat. "Bobby will be excited to hear that."

He stepped closer until they were toe to toe. "Just Bobby?"

She sniffed again. "I'm sure Mina and Farrah will throw you a party."

Mat's smile lit up the room. "I'll have to decline. There's someone else I'd much rather spend time with, if that's all right with you."

Luce's heart was about to burst. "Oh? Do I know her?"

Mat closed the little remaining distance between them and

captured her lips. The kiss stole her senses and seared itself onto her heart. When she came back to reality, she was wrapped around him and had to peel herself away.

"I think you know her pretty well," Mat said. The way he was looking at her made her blood surge. "Lucinda Garvey, will you be my non-pretend girlfriend?"

She tilted her head as if she was thinking about it before answering with an enthusiastic, "Yes!"

He swung her around the living room, and she didn't even hit anything as her legs flew out behind her.

"Just so you know," she said when her feet finally touched the ground. "I would love to see other parts of the world one day."

Mat touched his nose to hers. "And I can't wait to show them to you."

EPILOGUE

"SEE, I TOLD YOU," Delilah says, unwrapping a lemon pineapple marzipan gumdrop and popping it into her mouth. "They just needed a little push."

"I never doubted you," Charlotte says, still leaning around the kitchen door to spy on her brother and his girlfriend. "I just wasn't sure my brother would go for it."

"One-point-five billion data sets don't lie," Delilah reminds her. "Actually, I think we're up to 1.6 billion now. They're a cosmically perfect match, just like you and Micah."

Micah looks up from the sink full of dishes he's washing. "I don't really know if I buy into the whole cosmic data thing. But I'm glad anyway."

"As well you should be," Delilah replies. She thinks it's fun catching up with her former clients like this and enlisting their help.

Charlotte skips back into the room and picks up her dish towel to help with the drying. Delilah has been prohibited from helping anymore after disappearing the majority of Luce's parents' junk into a dimensional void. They'd said to get rid of it, so she'd gotten rid of it. If they hadn't wanted it transmogrified into a cube of atoms in another universe, they should have been more specific.

"So, are you taking off now? Gotten your next assignment yet?" Charlotte asks.

"I kind of like the candy store. I think I'll keep it a little longer and work with it as my home base. Oh, and I'll be training a new member of the Cupid Guild soon." She rubs her hands with delight at the thought of shaping a young mind. "Working in the human realm isn't as easy as it looks. I have a lot of wisdom to share."

Charlotte looks at Micah somewhat dubiously, but Delilah pretends she doesn't notice. She's come a long way and though this assignment was tricky, her case record is still unimpeachable.

Well, slightly impeachable, but she gets the job done. She can't wait to share her wisdom with her new apprentice.

Thank you for reading *The Cupid Guild*.
If you'd like more of my paranormal romance,
check out The Eternal Flame series.
Read on for an excerpt from book 1, *Angelborn*.

EXCERPT FROM ANGELBORN

MAIA

A groan escapes my throat as I enter my dorm room. *He* is here again. The strange one with the haunted eyes. There's just no way to win, is there?

My first year at Douglass University, my social worker, Rosie, pulled some strings and got me into the newest dorm, a building new enough that no one had died in it yet. And I had a single. For all of freshman year, my home was my sanctuary, but this year is different. I have a roommate, Genna. And she's got a dead guy haunting her.

If he were alive, most girls would call him hot. Light brown eyes, café au lait skin, close-cropped hair. He probably could have modeled in life. He looks about our age, but there's no way to tell how old he was when he died. The dead appear the way they remember themselves — it's not always how they looked at the end.

But this one is weird. He's kind of a failed hipster, all wannabe thrift-store chic in weird jeans and goofy T-shirts, but it totally doesn't work for him. And he floats, usually near the ceiling. That's pretty rare. I've seen a couple others who did stuff like that, but they're most often the really angry ones, like Natasha. The murder victims who are about to lose control. This guy seems calm. Harmless, even. He might actually be friendly, but I'm not planning on finding out. And he's completely obsessed with Genna. He hovers there, staring at her for hours. He's been here every day for the past week, since right after we moved in.

Rosie told me she'd checked Genna out. Both of her parents and all four of her grandparents are still alive, and she didn't seem to have any crazy exes in her past, certainly none who had died violently. No stalker types. She's lived a charmed life so far. She's a pretty girl, in a benign, friendly sort of way, and she's actually gone out of her way to be nice to me. Lord knows I haven't made it easy. Why she's being haunted, I have no idea, but it pisses me off.

When I walk in, Ghost Boy is, uncharacteristically, sitting at her desk. Genna is rifling through her dresser, looking for something. She's usually pretty neat — I guess Rosie checked that out about her too. I still organize her stuff when she's not around, but she hasn't said anything about it so far. It used to piss off Cadence, my roommate at the group home, but that never stopped me.

I drop onto my bed and am about to put in my headphones when Genna turns around.

"Caleb, meet Maia. Maia, Caleb." She points back and forth between me and her desk, then goes back to her dresser. Ghost Boy is staring right at me, but I avoid his eyes and look at Genna's back. I don't engage the dead anymore. Ignoring them has been working really well so far. And I know Genna can't see him, she never has before, so I have no idea what she's talking about. She slams her drawer shut, turns around, and smiles.

"She's kind of shy," she says.

I'm looking at her like she's crazy. Who the hell is she talking to? Her phone is on her desk, and she doesn't have a Bluetooth. Something about brain cancer.

Ghost Boy stands up directly in front of me, blocking my view, and holds out his hand like he expects me to shake it. Genna comes up beside him and lays a hand on his outstretched arm. I shoot off the bed, unable to peel my eyes away from her fingers brushing his arm. *She's touching him.* His skin looks normal. Golden hairs dust his forearm. His hand is still stretched out to me; I reach for it tentatively, brushing my fingers across warm human flesh before pulling my hand back as if stung.

I feel like I *have* been stung. Shocked by a cattle prod is more like it. I look back and forth from him to her, disbelief cutting off my airways. What. The. Fuck?

Genna's staring at me like I'm covered in green slime, and Ghost Boy's eyebrows are up to his forehead. I shake my head, trying to clear it. I can't take this. It's too fucked up.

I leave my stuff and run out of the room. Run until the dizziness engulfs me and I collapse.

Find ANGELBORN at http://lpen.co/angelborn

ABOUT THE AUTHOR

L. Penelope is an award-winning fantasy and paranormal romance author. Equally left and right-brained, she studied film-making and computer science in college and sometimes dreams in HTML. She lives in Maryland with her husband and furry dependents. Sign up for new release information, exclusives, and giveaways on her website: http://www.lpenelope.com.

ALSO BY L. PENELOPE

Earthsinger Chronicles

Song of Blood & Stone

Breath of Dust & Dawn

Whispers of Shadow & Flame

Hush of Storm & Sorrow

Cry of Metal & Bone

The Eternal Flame Series

Angelborn

Angelfall

www.ingramcontent.com/pod-product-compliance
Lightning Source LLC
Chambersburg PA
CBHW050520190726
48284CB00003B/877